Quintin Jardine is an independent public relations consultant and writer. He is the author of the highly acclaimed Skinner crime series as well as three further Oz Blackstone novels, *A Coffin for Two*, *Wearing Purple* and *Screen Savers*. He lives in East Lothian.

Praise for Quintin Jardine:

'If Ian Rankin is the Robert Carlyle of Scottish crime writers, then Jardine is surely its Sean Connery' *Heràld (Glasgow)*

'Deplorably readable' *Guardian*

'Engrossing, believable characters . . . captures Edinburgh beautifully . . . It all adds up to a very good read' *Edinburgh Evening News*

'Robustly entertaining' *Irish Times*

'Remarkably assured novel . . . a *tour de force*' *New York Times*

'Excellent thriller' *Manchester Evening News*

'Compelling stuff . . . one to watch' *Oxford Times*

Blackstone's Pursuits

Quintin Jardine

HEADLINE

First published in Great Britain in 1996
by HEADLINE BOOK PUBLISHING

First published in paperback in 1997
by HEADLINE BOOK PUBLISHING

A HEADLINE paperback

10 9 8 7 6 5 4 3 2

ISBN 0 7472 5460 5

Printed and bound in Great Britain by
Clays Ltd, St Ives plc

HEADLINE BOOK PUBLISHING
A division of Hodder Headline PLC
338 Euston Road
London NW1 3BH

This book is dedicated to the City of Edinburgh. (Sorry)

In which I stare death in the face, Uncle Hughie swamps the Yellow Peril, and McArse and I meet our match

Being a Private Enquiry Agent isn't all it's cracked up to be. In fact, there are some days when it cracks *me* up. And this was going to be one of those days, all right.

Quite a few of the people I'm sent to interview start out by being difficult. Many of them have a two-word vocabulary . . . if you know what I mean. It's as if they blame *me* for their wives having found out about them shagging that nice brunette person, or for their having been caught nicking a few quid from the partnership account.

This guy had done both, and I could tell at once that he was just not going to be the co-operative sort. It wasn't only that I'd walked in on him and caught him stark naked. My main problem was that the poor, sad bugger was stone dead.

Looking at him, stretched out on his back on the crumpled bed, I could tell that he had been a wee man, a bit closer to five feet than six. But equally, I could guess at once what the nice brunette had seen in him. People are always going on to me about my favourite adjectives. They say I use them for effect,

1

but that's not true. It's more that I take pleasure in words which strike me as particularly descriptive. At that moment, looking at him, stretched out on his back on the crumpled bed, '*disproportionate*' thrust itself to the front of my mind and lodged there.

The knife was impressive too. At least its big hilt was. The rest of it, the blade, was rammed up under the wee man's chin, nailing his mouth tight shut, away up behind his bulging eyes, all the way up, I guessed, into his brain.

Standing there, with the newly opened curtain still swinging behind me, I must have looked about as daft as he did. I stared at him, my eyes bulging out like organ-stops, just like his. He was ludicrous, lying there staring at the ceiling, so ludicrous that an idiot grin flickered around the corners of my mouth. Oddly, I felt myself feeling self-conscious, although why, God above knew. The wee man wasn't aware of anyone's presence, not any more, and his erstwhile companion was long gone.

It was the stench that drove home the enormity of it all. During my short, unhappy service as a probationer constable in Lothian and Borders Police I was called to the scene of precisely one death; yet another stupid kid found up a close in West Granton with a needle hanging out of her arm. My job had been to stand guard at the close-mouth, to keep a respectable distance between the wee girl – fifteen, she was, I remember – and the gawpers, oh yes, and between two bored, disinterested reporters who'd seen the same thing a few dozen times and who were pissed off because, but for this dead nuisance, they'd both have been freeloading at a civic lunch. The close-mouth was as close as I got to the victim, and until I walked into that room, that poor lassie was the only certifiably deceased person I'd ever seen.

At first, the shock shut out everything but the sight of him, but after a few seconds the hum forced its way up my nose. By and large, sphincters are a closed book to me, but not to the wee man on the bed. His had opened all of a sudden.

I turned back to the window, my stomach churning. The frames were the old wooden sash-cord type, the kind that usually you'd find stuck tight with paint. Thank Christ, though, once I'd freed the catch this one slid up nice and easy. I stuck my head out and took a deep breath, but it was no use. Normally, old Uncle Hughie eases up on you, giving you a couple of nudges so that you can be in the right place when finally he puts in an appearance. Not this time. The old familiar fist gripped my belly and squeezed as hard as it could, forcing up everything in there in a single violent shout, and firing it on to the pavement fifteen feet below. Well, almost on to the pavement. Instead of a splash, there was a yell.

'Whit the . . . Away, ya dirty bastard!'

My eyes were still shut tight from the effort of my mighty boak. I opened one of them, fearfully, and looked down into Ebeneezer Street. The flat top of the traffic warden's cap, and the shoulders of his tunic had caught most of it, but I was pleased to see – it's funny, the details the mind registers in times of crisis – that some of Uncle Hughie's output had landed on the page of his notebook on which the Yellow Peril was noting down the details of my out-of-date tax disc.

I opened the other eye and looked at him, pleading. 'Aw come on, man! It only expired last week.'

He stared up at me, sending the mess on his hat cascading down the back of his heavy, porous uniform. 'Yellow Peril' had never been a more fitting nickname.

'Whit's the game, Jimmy?' He didn't have the wit to be astonished, only angry.

3

'Lamb Rogan Josh,' I muttered. 'From the takeaway in Caroline Street. Sorry!' I decided that I preferred the sight on the bed. Besides, the traffic warden probably smelled even worse than him. I pulled my head back into the room. As I did, I felt a current of cool air on my face and realised that I must have left the front door open. I walked out of the room and into the hall to close it.

I almost felt offended when she didn't scream. I mean, isn't that what women are supposed to do when they step into their flat and find a six-foot stranger standing in the lobby, even if he is wearing a Savoy Tailors' Guild suit and holding a Motorola cell-phone in his hand?

When I got round to asking her, she really did offend me. 'You just looked terrified,' she said. 'I felt sorry for you.' I could have handled it if she'd said that fear had struck her dumb, or even just plain surprise. I could even have lived with revulsion. But being told I was pitiful was as hurtful as a smart kick on the kneecap, and the effect lasted longer.

In the there and then of it, she just stood and looked at me, her big brown eyes not startled, not even slightly wide, just questioning. She wore faded jeans, a crumpled tee-shirt and trainers with more than a few miles on the odometer. The bag slung over her shoulder looked bigger than she was. She let it slip to the floor as she shut the door behind her. In her right hand she held a bunch of keys big enough to choke a horse.

'Well?' she said, and I could have sworn she was smiling. 'Are you him, then?'

I looked back at her: blankly, I think. 'Eh?' Right at that moment that was all the articulacy I could manage.

'The mystery man. Dawn's wee bit of illicit rough.'

The hair at the back of my neck prickled. This was like stepping into the middle of someone else's movie. I decided

4

that I'd better get a grip on reality, double-quick.

'Look, I'm sorry. My name's Oz Blackstone. I'm a private enquiry agent. I work for lawyers, insurance companies and the like.

'I had an appointment to meet someone here this morning, at ten o'clock. When I got here, the door was unlocked. I knocked, and it just swung open. I shouted, but there was no answer. I thought that was odd, so I stepped inside and took a look around.' I pulled a card from the stash in the breast pocket of my jacket. 'Here.'

She looked at it. 'Oz, eh. You don't sound like an Australian.'

I scowled at her. Always, the same wisecrack. I sighed, and gave her the stock answer. 'I'm not. It's just that Osbert doesn't cut the mustard down Pilton way.'

She gave me an odd smile, with a *touché* look about it. 'I know what you mean. My name's Prim Phillips. It's short for "Primavera". In English that means "Springtime". I was conceived in May, on a holiday in a tent in the Costa Brava, and my Maw's a terrible romantic. I decided early on that there was no bloody way I was going through life answering to "Vera", therefore . . . You and I are kindred spirits in the daft name stakes.' She shook her tousled sun-bleached head and smiled, and flashed me the sort of look that doesn't stop at your eyes, but drills right into your head. 'Imagine,' she said, 'giving a wee girl a four-syllable name!'

She picked up the huge bag. 'Hold on till I stick this in the bedroom. Then you can tell me the rest of your story.'

I stepped between her and the door. She frowned, and for the first time, looked just a touch apprehensive. I tried to sound cool and reassuring, but it came out flustered and panicky. 'Don't go in there, Miss Phillips. I said there was no reply; I didn't say that there wasn't anyone here.'

5

She was afraid now. 'Dawn . . .' she began. She tried to push past me, but I gripped her arms and held her. It wasn't easy. She's a strong wee package.

'No, it isn't Dawn . . . unless she's balding and helluva well hung.' See me, see gallows humour! She looked at me, twisting against my grip and wincing. I realised that the Motorola was digging into her arm, and let her go. 'Sorry!'

'That's my bedroom. I want to see what's in there,' she said. 'However bad it is, I've seen worse. Come on.' There was something in her voice which told me that 'Don't,' would always be the wrong thing to say to this woman. I tried, 'Are you sure?' instead, but that didn't work either.

'Okay,' I said finally. 'But don't get the wrong idea about me when you see in there.' She looked at me, incredulously.

When I got round to asking her whether, finding two strangers in her flat, one with a head like a kebab and the other heading for the door, it hadn't occurred to her for a second that the live one might have had something to do with the dead one being dead, she offended me again. 'Don't be daft, Oz. I've met people who could do that sort of thing. You couldn't, not in a month of Sundays, not if your life depended on it.' It can do something to your manhood when a slip of a woman looks you in the eye and tells you that you don't have the stuff to be a cold-blooded killer.

Back in the there and then of it, she stood beside the bed, looking down at the wee man. 'That's got to be him, all right. Dawn's bit of illicit. She said in her last letter that he was built like a cross between Danny deVito and Nijinsky. I thought she meant the dancer, not the horse!'

His hands were by his sides. She leaned over and lifted one up. 'Been dead for a while,' she said. 'He's cold, and the rigor's beginning to wear off. When did you find him?'

I glanced at my watch, embarrassed by the tremble of my hand. It was almost ten-thirty. 'About half an hour ago.'

All of a sudden I couldn't take it, all that coolness in the face of crisis. 'Look, Miss Phillips, Prim, whatever: what is it with you? You walk into your flat and you find a strange guy knifed to death in your bed, and you're standing here as if it's just something that the cleaner's missed. What sort of a world do you live in?' My voice rose as I spoke, and suddenly there was a crack in it that I'd thought I lost in my teens.

She took me by the arm and led me out of the room, through the hall and into a narrow kitchen. 'Sit down, Oz.' There were two chairs, one on either side of a gate-leg table. She picked up a white plastic kettle and filled it from the mixer tap over the sink, then switched it on. She lifted a jar marked 'Tea' and shook it. Turning, she bent her back against the work-surface and looked down at me, as the kettle began to hiss and bubble behind her.

'I'm a nurse. I've just spent a year in a refugee camp in Central Africa, in the middle of a tribal war zone. When I say I've seen worse than that in there, I'm not kidding.

'On top of that, I've just spent the last umpteen hours wide awake in aeroplanes. All I wanted, when I came in here was a shower, a vodka and tonic, and a sleep. Instead, I've got a slightly hysterical private eye in my kitchen and a corpse in my bed. If my reaction seems odd to you, it's because all this is a dream; because none of it's happening.

'It's also because I'm trying not to imagine where my sister is, or how she's involved with what's through next door.

'That's me. Now, before we do anything else, what's your story?' She turned her back on me as the kettle boiled and set about the business of making tea. I sat there, bewildered and dumb.

She looked over her shoulder. 'Well?'

I stood up, in a feeble attempt to assert myself. I searched for something smart to say, but all I could manage was a shrug of the shoulders. She handed me a mug of tea. It reminded me of the dark, hot, sweet char that was my Granny Blackstone's standard remedy for shock, exposure, skinned knees, a wee touch of the flu and a host of other conditions up to and including mild coronary incidents. My Granny's tea was a wonderful brew. Apart from its therapeutic value, she used it to dye Easter Eggs, and swore by it as a tanning agent. She used to keep it cold in a jar, and slabber it on herself every time the sun poked its nose into the back court. She was found one day, dead in her deckchair. My Dad reckoned that she'd finally pickled herself.

I took a sip of Prim's version. It was sweet, as I'd expected, yet different. I took a deeper swallow, and felt it go to work, stilling the trembling in my arms and legs. 'Nice,' I said. 'What's in it?'

'A spoonful of honey. Better for you than sugar. Now, come on. Let's hear it.'

'Okay.' I took a deep breath. 'Like I said, I work for lawyers and insurers in the main. Taking statements from witnesses in court cases and so on. This commission was a wee bit different. A few days ago I was called in by the senior partner of a firm of stockbrokers called Black and Muirton. I'd heard of them, but I tend to do my investing through bookmakers. The guy, Archer, he's called, said to me that they had a problem with one of their partners.

'It seems that their practice accountant found some heavy irregularities in the books. The firm keeps an offshore bank account in Jersey for holding clients' money on a short-term basis, when it buys and sells for them. Cash goes flying through it all the time, very serious cash sometimes, because it's a big firm with some high-roller clients, plus, they handle business for banks and fund managers. What the audit found was that the account didn't balance. In fact it was off balance by nine hundred thousand squigglies.

'It took them a while but eventually they tracked it down. The cash had come from the sale of some loan stock held by one of their multi-millionaire clients. It had been transferred, electronically, to a numbered bank account in Switzerland. The sale had been authorised, and the transfer made, by one of the partners, a Mr William Kane. The trouble was, there was nothing on Black and Muirton's records to show that the client had instructed it, and nothing to show that the bank account was his.

'Archer pulled some strings in Switzerland. He found out that the account was opened by a Scots woman called Dawn Phillips. It was a real cloak and dagger job. When she set it up she showed the Swiss people half of a Bank of Scotland fiver, serial number AF 426469. Her instructions were that access was to be given to any two people who showed up with both halves of that same note.'

Prim nodded. 'That sounds right up my sister's street. She was the only wee girl I've ever known to ask for an Action Man for Christmas. She was reading James Bond by the time she was ten. There was no way she was ever going to grow up to be anything but an actress.'

Quite a family, I thought, Mother Teresa and Madonna in the same brood. 'Some part she's playing this time, then,' I said. 'Guess what happened next? While Archer was trying to figure out what to do, Mrs Kane dropped in on Mrs Archer and poured her heart out. She said that William had been keeping some odd hours. They've been married for twelve years, and

9

she could set her watch by him. But all of a sudden he started working late at the office on pretty much a nightly basis, and having to go off and see clients at the weekend.

'Like any sensible wife she started to go through his pockets on the quiet, and found the usual. Ticket stubs for two at UCI, credit-card slips for hotel bills in Inverness when he was meant to be in London and so on. She fronted him up but he just told her she was being silly. Then one day she got home from the shops and there was a "Dear Joan" note on the kitchen table, telling her that he had met this wonderful girl called Dawn, and sorry as he was, that was it.

'To cut it short, Mrs Archer told Mr Archer and he had Kane into his office. He confronted him with the sale order and told him the story about the Swiss account. Kane admitted the lot. He told him that he had fallen truly, madly, deeply in love with your sister, and that he had come up with this daft scheme because he knew his wife would cut the nuts off him financially. His idea was to leave her to it and to shoot the craw with Dawn and the nine hundred thou.

'Archer reckoned that he was completely off his trolley. He told him to bail out while he thought up Plan A, but to leave an address where he could be contacted, and a telephone number. He did. Yours.'

Prim puffed up with indignation. 'The cow! I let her use this place while I was away on the basis that I didn't want any bloke's shaving tackle in my bathroom.'

'That's the least of your worries. Those sheets of yours are definitely a goner, and I don't think the mattress'll be too clever either.'

She wrinkled her nose. 'Ugh! Thanks, Oz. I was trying not to think about that.' Wrinkled or not, as noses go it was a right wee cracker. It set her brown eyes off a treat, and didn't bully her perfect mouth either. I realised that I was beginning to feel myself again.

'So what happened next?' she asked. 'What brought you here?'

'Archer sent me. He called me as soon as Kane was out of the office. By that time he was shitting himself about the good name of the firm. You know what a village Edinburgh is. One whiff of the unsavoury and his client list would disappear like snow off a dyke in August. He'd decided that the only thing for it was to get that nearly million back into the client's account and to spin him a line about crystallising capital gains for him, or some such stuff like that.

'He told me to go and see Kane, to get both halves of the fiver from him, then to get my arse over to Switzerland with some close-mouthed helper, and bring back the lolly. He promised me a five per cent success fee. To spare you the mental arithmetic, that's forty-five grand. For me, more than a year's wages in one hit.

'I phoned your number last night. A woman answered; I guessed it must have been Dawn. She put me on to Kane, I told him what the score was and he said "Yes sir, very good, sir. Come here at ten tomorrow morning, and I'll give you the bank-note." That's us up to date.

'I've never seen Kane, not even a photograph, but I'm assuming that's him through there on your bed. Unless your sister's lying under it in the same condition, then it looks as if you're in for a family scandal.' Her face twisted in pain, and I bit my tongue, to punish it for running away with itself, like always.

'That's your theory, Mr Detective, is it?'

'Prim,' I said, 'I'm a private enquiry agent, not a detective. I interview witnesses in court cases for lawyers, and that sort of stuff. I was a policeman for six months, once upon a time, and I turned it in because I couldn't stand the Clever Bastards in the CID, and the bullying sergeants in uniform who'd spent the best part of their service sitting on their brains.

'But what I said there, I'm sorry, but it's the first thing they'll think. No, it's the *only* thing they'll think. If these blokes see any easy answer, they don't spend a hell of a lot of time looking for a difficult option. They're not trained to be clever, they're trained to be logical.'

The old tongue was really running away with itself now. I suppose I could have stopped it, but I wasn't prepared to bite it that hard.

'Look Prim, I find it difficult to believe that anyone could do something like that next door, especially someone with a sister as . . .' I gulped, but I had run straight off the cliff, like Wiley E. Coyote, and all I could do was keep on running and hope that I didn't hit the ground. '. . . as downright tasty as you, but the boys and girls from the Leith Polithe won't dithmith the idea. And like it or not, we're going to have to call them.'

She nodded. Her blonde hair was cut fairly short, and more than a bit untidy after her journey. Suddenly I found myself wanting to smooth it.

'I know we are,' she said, 'but how about if we have a shooftie round to see if we can find that fiver before we do? Your clients would like that, wouldn't they.' Until that moment, I'd never grasped what 'askance' meant, but when I looked at Prim, I knew for sure. 'Well,' she said, picking up my expression. 'If it's there, all of it, it'll mean that Dawn . . . and we don't know for sure she was here . . . didn't kill him for the money. Won't it?'

I saw the sense in that. But I saw even more in the forty-five thousand good reasons I had for wanting to find the fiver too. 'Aye, okay. Let's look, at least.'

Policemen are like buses. When you need one, they're now-here to be found. But when you don't . . .

I'll never know why anyone could call a game 'Postman's Knock'. I mean, when it comes to knocking there's no-one in the same league as a polisman. We had just stepped out of the kitchen when the thump on the door echoed around the hall. Prim's flat was on the first floor of the tenement. I'll swear that I heard at least three doors open as the sound swept through the building. She stepped up to the door and peered through the spy-hole.

'It looks like a traffic warden,' she said. 'But his uniform . . . !' The second knock sent her reeling backwards. 'Okay,' she shouted. 'Keep your hair on.' She swung the door open. The be-fouled traffic warden was there, all right, flanked on either side by two of Edinburgh's finest. One of them, I recognised. When I did my probationer spell at Oxgangs he had been the senior constable and chief barrack-room lawyer at the station. He was one of those guys who was determined to see it out to pension time and sod all the rest. Wherever they go they infect the whole station, whingeing and bitching until they've pulled morale down to rock bottom. Eventually they're rotated to start all over somewhere else. This one's name was McArthur, but at Oxgangs everyone, from the Chief Inspector down, had called him McArse.

His sidekick could have been me seven years earlier. He was a fuzz-cheeked probationer, so spick that I guessed his Maw still did his laundry, and so span that I guessed she pressed his uniform for him as well. I shook my head at the thought of what could happen to the poor wee bugger on the beat in Leith.

13

McArse stared right over Prim's head, straight at me. I could see something stirring behind his eyes, but his sort have trouble putting a name to their chief constable, let alone a short-serving wet-ear from almost a decade earlier. He gave up as soon as he started and went straight into Chapter One of the training manual, 'The Policeman as a Public Servant'.

'Hey, youse. Mister. What the fuck about this then?' He thrust Exhibit A into the hall, with the evidence of the outrage drying on his cap and shoulders. '*Another fine mess you've got yourself into, Oz*,' I thought.

When you're as thick as McArse very few things will stem the tide of your aggression, far less rock you back on your heels. The only one I know that works every time is a counterblast from a small, furious woman. When the woman in question has just stepped off a transcontinental flight minus a night's sleep, after twelve months in the middle of a genocidal African war, well it really is no contest.

From behind I could see her shoulders quiver as she surveyed the soiled public official before her. The warden stood there, wishing suddenly that, rather than stopping the first idiot he had encountered with flat feet and a black and white check band round his cap, he had made his way quietly back to his depot, to blame the incident on a large family of incontinent seagulls, attracted by the shine of a car he was booking.

'Constable!' hissed Prim. A good hiss is far more effective than a bellow, any time. 'Get this apparition out of my flat, at once, and take a grip on your manners.' McArse looked at her, noticing her for the first time. The ponderous wheels of his brain weighed up the situation for a few seconds, until without a word, he took the quailing warden by the collar and drew him backwards out on to the stairhead.

'That's better,' she said.

When I was a kid, if I was ever bullied, I used to get my big sister to sort it out. Standing there behind Prim, I felt a wave of *déjà vu* sweeping over me. 'Look pal,' I said to the warden, more from a need to assert my independence as a man – or even my presence – than from any wish to appease the thing, 'accidents will happen, okay. Sorry and all that.'

Prim looked at me over her shoulder, incredulous again. I made a face that was intended to say, 'Look I don't normally throw up at crime scenes, and even less frequently over traffic wardens, but the smell in there just got to me all of a sudden. Okay?' That's what it was meant to say, but it didn't work. Incredulity stayed in place, until it was replaced by one of my big sister's playground looks, the one she would throw me just before she put the boot into the Primary Three class bully. It said very clearly, 'You can explain yourself later!' Oddly, I felt a surge of delight when I caught the 'later'.

She turned back to the odd trio in the doorway and pulled off a masterful role switch. 'Yes Constable, we're sorry, but you see, the most terrible thing's happened. We were just about to call the police.

'I'm just back from abroad. My boyfriend picked me up from the airport. When we got in he went into the bedroom and he found . . .' From somewhere, she conjured up a sob. 'You'd better look for yourselves.' She pointed behind her to the door.

McArse was no better with a tearful woman than with an angry one. He nudged the probationer. 'Gaun, Jason . . .' '*Bugger me*,' I thought. '*He's called Jason!*' '. . . away and take a look.' He glowered at the traffic warden who had led him into this pit of torment. 'You! You can go. Ye're stinkin' the place oot onywey.' The Yellow, Orange and Slightly Pink Peril slunk

15

off, out of the picture forever. McArse gave the reluctant boy Jason a shove towards the bedroom.

I *know*. I should have said something. I'd been in the boy's shoes once, yet I let him walk unwarned into that bedroom. Rotten bastard, eh? 'Fraid so.

Unlike me, Jason didn't throw up. Mind you, I'd take throwing up every time rather than what he did. A low, keening sound came from the room. A wailing 'Oooowwhhh,' which grew in intensity and distress, the sound of knees and thighs being squeezed tight together in a fruitless effort to prevent the inevitable.

'Ooohh!'

In the doorway the old soldier pretended not to hear. He stood there like Pharaoh trying, in the midst of the Red Sea, to ignore the fact that something very significant was happening to the water table – an apt comparison in the circumstances.

'Hector.' The call came from the room. If you've ever wondered about 'tremulous', that was it. The veteran looked at the ceiling.

'Hector!' Slightly more urgent this time. 'And whereabouts were you abroad, Miss?' the reluctant visitor asked Prim.

'McArse!' It was a howl from Hell. 'Get fuckin' in here!' Shocked into movement, the constable lumbered through the hall and into the bedroom. Five seconds later, he backed out white-faced.

'Oh my God, Miss. Was he like that when you found him?'

I almost said, 'No, you stupid bastard, he was alive!' but decided that silence was a better option. Prim had figured that one out too; she nodded meekly.

The probationer Jason eased himself awkwardly out of the bedroom, trying desperately not to look at anyone. I didn't have the heart to ask if he was all right, because I could see that he wasn't. I could recognise a career cut short when I saw one. I let him go as he shuffled along the hall and out to the stairhead.

At last, McArse, from somewhere, dredged up the memory of what it was like to be a policeman. 'Where's your phone, Miss?' he asked, quietly. The one thing that keeps guys like him alive in the force is their knack of knowing when to delegate, upwards or downwards, and that is just as often as they can.

Prim and I retreated silently to the flat's small living room as he went into the kitchen to phone.

'Why did you say that about getting back from the airport?' I asked her.

She looked at me. Shyness sat oddly on her. 'I don't know. It just came out. I suppose I thought it would be awkward for you if I told them what really happened. I mean your client's secret would be out and everything.'

'Aye, and I'd be in the frame as Obvious Culprit Number One.' She smiled. She didn't say 'Hardly.' She didn't need to.

Instead, she said, 'What happens now?'

I shrugged. 'The serious boys arrive. The CID. The Clever Bastards with absolutely no sense of humour. Not a bit like those two out there. Look, Prim, we're going to have to be straight with them. Nothing held back. What I mean is you're going to have to tell them that Dawn was living here.'

'We'll see.' Somehow, that didn't reassure me.

In which Dylan gets the blues,
we get lucky and I seize my chance

The Clever Bastards who turned up were from Leith CID. Ebeneezer Street was only a short hop from their station and so we heard rubber burning on the road outside less than five minutes after McArse's call.

The officer who burst into the living room might as well have had 'High Flyer' stamped on his forehead. He radiated ambition as he looked down at us, sat together on the couch facing the window. Guys like him can be very dangerous. Turn them loose on a criminal investigation, especially one that's heading for the High Court and the tabloids, and they don't see people, they see rungs on the ladder of success.

I knew his face from the wine bars and fancy pubs around Charlotte Square, but not his name. He filled in the blank in my knowledge at once. 'I'm DI Michael Dylan. The plate on the door says Phillips. Is that both of you?'

Prim shook her head. 'No, it's my place. We don't live together.' '*You're telling the truth, Prim,*' I thought. '*Careful, that could be dangerous.*'

She squeezed my arm. I don't know whether she meant to dig her thumbnail into my wrist, but if she did, it was unnecessary. I'd learned enough about Primavera Phillips in our short acquaintance to be happy to let her lead the dance. I sat there dumb. 'This is Oz Blackstone, my boyfriend,' she said. I did my best to look gormless. From Dylan's expression, I succeeded.

For a DI he looked pretty young. Early thirties, I guessed, not much older than me. He was a real designer polisman, dressed in an olive-green suit that looked like Armani, and with his feet encased in tan leather shoes that definitely were not made for pounding the beat. Someone once said to me that Dylan saw himself as a bit of a cult, and that most of his colleagues agreed . . . only they spelled it differently.

Everything about him said that he was aiming for the Command Suite, and the predatory look in his eye told me that he could see Prim and me helping him on his way.

He didn't disappoint me. 'How about making it easy for me?' he said. 'The way I see it, honey, you set the wee chap up. You lure him to this place with promises of unbridled passion. You've got him gasping for it and helpless, then Oz here comes in and knifes him.

'All you really need to tell me is what you were after. Was it money, or is this a contract job? The rest is pretty obvious.'

'Mmm,' said Prim. 'Indeed.' There was a long, dangerous silence. Dylan looked down, all smugness and expectancy. 'And having done that,' she went on, softly, but with an edge to her voice that made me think of a demolition ball swinging unstoppably towards its target, 'the cold-eyed hitman here went and barfed out the window all over a traffic warden? Yes?

'Then, after that mishap, the death squad hung about the

scene until PC Murdoch and Oor Wullie arrived.'

She stood up and squared up to the Armani suit and its contents, which suddenly seemed a touch less sure of themselves. 'Let me tell you a few things, Mr Dylan. First, this is my flat, that ruined bed next door is mine, and I'm not happy about it. Second, no way would I let a thing like that through there anywhere near me.' I wasn't quite sure which thing she meant, the whole or the part. I guessed, she meant the latter, and felt a lot better about life, manhood, and associated issues. 'Third, if you care to repeat that allegation before independent witnesses, Oz and I will sue you right out of that suit.'

I sat there on the couch, staring at Prim's bum in her tight, faded jeans. It was a nice, round bum, generously fleshed but firm. I tried to imagine her committing acts of unbridled passion upon the person of the late William Kane, but somehow I wound up taking his place, with a bridle figuring somewhere in the scene, too. Eventually I forced myself to look up at Clever Bastard Dylan. He stood there, his face working itself into a cheesy grin as he fought to protect his dignity. 'Okay,' he said, finally. 'Just testing. Have you any idea who that is, through there?'

She looked him dead in the eye. 'Neither Oz or I have ever seen that man before in our lives.'

He missed the fact that she hadn't answered his question. 'Okay. The constable said you got back from the airport and found the body?'

'Yes,' said Prim. She dug into her vast bag and produced a boarding card. 'There.' She thrust it at Dylan. 'That's the flight I was on. Eight o'clock shuttle. It was a bit late so Oz and I didn't get back here till after ten.' He bought the lie without question.

21

'The guy in there's been dead since last night.'

'Oh, you know a lot about bodies do you?' Dylan was the sort of prat who patronises women automatically. This time he didn't even realise he was doing it until the axe of Prim's sarcasm fell on his neck.

'I'm afraid I do. I've seen all sorts over the last twelve months. A few days ago, in fact, we went into a village and found a policeman with his testicles in his mouth. Just as well for his sake that *he* was dead. I mean what good's a policeman without . . .'

Quite suddenly, she began to sob. '*Thank Christ*,' I thought, relieved that she wasn't *that* tough. I stood up and turned her towards me, holding her like the concerned partner I was supposed to be. 'There, love,' I said, warming to the part. 'You had a hell of a time out in Africa. A dead stranger in your bed's the last thing you needed to come home to.'

I glared at Dylan. He was completely conquered now. 'Look, Mr . . . eh Blackstone, was it? Why don't you look after Miss Phillips. My people will just have a look round . . . if that's all right, that is?'

'Aye, sure. You get on with it.'

I expected Prim to break the clinch when the door closed behind him, but she hung on in there. Her sobs were subsiding, but every so often a fresh outbreak would set her generous chest rubbing against my belly. Remembering that she had been a stranger an hour before, I racked my brains for images which would distract me and kill the reflex which Prim's bra-less nipples were triggering in me. I thought of Hibernian defending a one-goal lead on a wet Saturday in January. I thought of an evening at the ballet with a woman I didn't like. I thought of the bit in *Pulp Fiction* where John Travolta shoots Marvin in the face by accident. I thought of

22

Van Morrison. I thought of a bottle of duty-free Grolsch after midnight on a cross-channel ferry.

None of it worked. Before she could get the wrong idea, which would have been right all along, I held her away from me at arm's length. 'Come on Prim. There'll be time for that later.' She looked back at me tear-stained, and nodded. It's funny how there are people you can know for an hour and it seems like a lifetime.

'Yes, you're right. That prick'll be back.' ('*You never know*,' I thought mischievously to myself.) 'I'll need to work out a story that'll protect Dawn, as far as I can.'

Dylan must have had a pressing lunch date, because the prick was back within fifteen minutes. 'The Doc's arrived,' he said. 'Her first estimate is that he was killed between ten and midnight last night by a right-handed man. If you're up to it now, Miss Phillips, perhaps you could clear up just one or two things.'

Prim nodded.

'How long have you been in Africa?'

'A year.'

'And you don't have a key, Mr Blackstone?'

'No, he doesn't. Nor do I to Oz's place. That implies a permanent commitment, and we're not ready for that.' '*Speak for yourself*,' I thought, falling deeper in love by the minute.

'So who's been using your flat while you've been away.'

'I have a sister,' said Prim. She sounded casual, but I knew she was measuring every word. 'She's an actress. She never knows where her next job'll be, so she doesn't have a place of her own. She sleeps on my couch or rooms with other performers when she's in town. Sometimes her friends crash down here too. When I left I gave her a key and said that she could let her crowd use it as long as they kept it clean and didn't smoke dope.

'You could say that this flat's been a sort of doss-house for luvvies for the last twelve months. I've got no idea who might have been here last night. And as for the bloke next door, I told you I've never seen him before.'

'How about you, Mr Blackstone?' said Dylan quickly, with a failed attempt at slyness.

I was ready for him. 'As Prim said, me neither.' I chanced my arm. 'Do you know who he is?'

Dylan shook his head. 'His wallet seems to have been taken. There's nothing there to identify him.' He looked down again at Prim. 'We've found some keys in the kitchen, Miss. Could you have a look at them to see if the one you gave your sister's among them?'

He led us back across the hall. In the kitchen, a leaf of the table had been raised, and various objects were spread on it. Half a dozen keys of various sorts. An empty pill bottle. A five pound note, serial number AF 426469, cut into two halves.

She didn't break stride, catch her breath or anything else. She looked at the keys carefully. 'These two are for the coalshed down in the back yard. These two are for my parents' place. That one's for the Yale in the front door. The other fitted a lock I had changed when I moved in here.' She picked up the pill bottle. I leaned over and sneaked a quick look. The label read 'Prozac: Miss D. Phillips.' She picked up the two halves of the fiver and looked round at Dylan. 'You found my secret stash, then. Very thorough!'

Dylan looked embarrassed and nodded at a pile of muesli heaped on the floor, surrounded by the shattered pieces of a ceramic container. 'Sorry about that, Miss. One of these clumsy sods knocked it off the counter. We can replace it if you like.'

'That's all right,' said Prim. 'I never liked it anyway. I'll use this to buy another, one that doesn't break this time.' Casually, she slipped the two halves of the note into the pocket of her jeans.

'Why did you cut it?' asked Dylan.

'Added security,' she replied, mysteriously.

'What else can we do, Inspector,' she asked, ingenuously.

Dylan shrugged his shoulders. 'I'd like you both to call into the Police Station in Queen Charlotte Street to give us formal statements, but tomorrow'll be fine for that. Make it around midday.'

We each nodded. 'So when,' asked Prim, 'will you be finished here?'

The Inspector sucked his teeth. 'Hard to say, Miss. Depends on the technicians. They'll want to pick up every hair and every piece of fluff from that bedroom, so we can match it to a suspect, sooner or later. Don't you worry about that, we'll get him.

'I shouldn't reckon they'll be any more than a couple of days.'

'Two days!' She puffed up like a pigeon in her indignation. 'What the hell am I going to . . .'

I seized her hand, and my chance. 'What the hell else are you going to do? Let's take your kit round to my place and leave these guys to it.'

In which Jan gets a shock,
Primavera meets Wallace,
and I gain a sleeping partner.

O ut in the street, I was delighted to see that the Traffic
Warden from the Other Side had been so disconcerted
that he had neglected to paste me up for my out-of-date disc.
The blue Nissan wore no adornment other than bird-shit, and
a few specks that weren't.

I opened the tailgate door and slung Prim's kitbag first into
the boot, and then the smaller one which she had packed with
a few 'sensible clothes' from her wardrobe and cupboard,
under the supervision of a young woman detective, who, she
told me, had kept sneaking astounded glances at the tiny
colossus on the bed.

Neither of us spoke as I coaxed the engine into life and
reversed out of my parking space. I weaved my way through
the police cars which were thronging the street like ants round
a peach-stone. We were heading up Leith Walk, when Prim
said: 'So where is it then? This refuge I'm bound for, this pad
of yours.'

I grinned, thinking it would put her at ease. From her

expression, my grin must have been more of a leer. 'Not that far. It's in the Old Town, down one of the closes off the High Street.'

'And will Mrs Blackstone be gone for long?'

'My mother is dead,' I said solemnly.

Prim frowned. 'Don't be cheap. You know what I mean, Mrs as in spouse, or even Ms Something Else as in live-in partner.'

I shook my head. 'I don't have any of those. My last live-in girlfriend was two years ago. She died of "dish-pan hands, Mummy", or so she said. Since then I've preferred my independence. There are some bloody good takeaways around the centre of town, you know.' I let the silence fill the car as she weighed up Oz in a new environment, and pondered the prospect of Oz on Oz's turf.

'Mind you,' I said, after a suitable interval, looking sheepishly at the dashboard as we turned into Leith Walk. 'I don't know how you'll take to Wallace.'

She gasped. 'Wallace! You're not . . .'

I relished the sight of Prim on the back foot. 'What about it if I am?' She looked at me, uncertain for the first time in our short acquaintance.

'Actually, if there was anything between Wallace and me they'd have to invent a new name for it. Wallace is an Iguana. He's the last of the dinosaurs. I named him after a wizened old fisherman uncle of my Mum's.'

Her jaw dropped. 'Let me get this right. You're taking me to a flat that you share with a lizard?'

'Wallace would be hurt by the description, but yes, that just about sums it up.'

She threw back her head and laughed. 'The first time I saw you, Oz Blackstone, I thought there might be some mileage in you. Could be I was right.'

28

'I'm touched, my dear.'

'Yes, that was what I thought.'

'Thank you again, on behalf of loonies everywhere. But seriously for once, we're clear of that lot back there. Is there anywhere else you want me to take you? How about your parents?'

'God no, Oz. For a start they're in Auchterarder; and for seconds, sooner or later Mum would ask me about Dawn, and I've never been able to lie to her.'

'But Prim, you're going to need to talk to her. The murder might be reported on telly tonight. She could see your flat on the news.'

She shook her head slowly. 'No, I think not. My parents cling to this planet by their fingertips. Mother's hobby is Romantic Novels and Dad devotes his life to making model soldiers. He sells them to collectors through magazines. Anything from one-off Kilties to whole battle scenes, to order. They're just not interested in what's on the telly, unless it's by Barbara Taylor Bradford or Kate Adie.'

'Is there anyone else, then?' Suddenly I was seized by the thought that taking this woman under my roof would be the biggest step into the unknown that I'd ever made. 'Do you have any friends in Edinburgh?'

She turned in her seat and looked at me. 'Do I feel the chill of cold feet? Do you want to be shot of me?'

'Absolutely not,' I shot back at her, too fast in the circumstances. 'I just don't want you to feel that you're being . . .'

'Spirited away to your lair, were you going to say?' Her smile was delicious. 'Don't worry, Oz, we fell into this thing together, and I reckon we should see it through together. More than that, you're my best bet for a shower and a sleep. Shower first, though. Do I need one!'

I creased my nose and looked sideways at her. 'Funny that. I was just thinking that it's been a long time since I had a really ripe woman in this car!' She slapped my arm, hard enough for me to feel her strength, not hard enough to hurt. I saw her tanned nurse's bicep bunch.

We made our way up the Walk, pausing occasionally for red lights. It was a beautiful warm day in early May, and the trees in the central reservation were in blossom.

'You know, Mr Oz Blackstone,' said Prim, 'this may sound like the wrong thing to say in the circumstances, but I'm glad to be home. Even Florence Nightingale must have become de-humanised after a while. If you need an example, just think back to how I reacted to finding a corpse in my bed!'

'Hey,' I said as gently as I could. 'You *are* home. Just hang on to that. You're in Edinburgh and it's beautiful. Look around you.' The car swept round the Elm Row island, and up towards Picardy Place. She laughed. 'Come on Oz. That's the St James Centre up ahead. Not even a homeboy could call that beautiful.'

'Okay, well just hang on a minute. We'll get to some nice bits!'

My house is in one of the nicer bits. Less than half a mile from the Palace of Holyroodhouse, so for a week every year I can say that I have the Queen for a neighbour.

'What's this?' said Prim, as I slid the Nissan into my parking space.

'My house. Where I live. It's a conversion. It used to be a grain store or something, until a developer got hold of it. I live in that pointy bit up there. It's more of a loft than a flat. See the bit right at the top? According to the estate agent who sold me the place, that's called a belvedere. There's a ladder up to it. Quite often Wallace climbs up it to sun himself. Yes, there

30

he is, look.' As if wakened by the sound of our arrival, the iguana peered down at us solemnly.

'Jesus,' said Prim, shaking her head. 'I find a dead dwarf in my bed, and now I'm going home with a guy who has an iguana as a flatmate.'

'A loft, not a flat,' Must get the terminology right.

'Loft, flat,' she said. 'What's the difference?'

'About five grand in a good market, I reckon.' That got her attention.

We made our way up the narrow, twisty stairway to my pad, and stepped into the tiny square area which passed for my entrance hall. Two doors and a staircase led from it. 'Kitchen to the left, bathroom door to the right,' I said. I opened each door to demonstrate. When I opened the door on the right, a red-faced woman screamed. She was sat on the toilet, so it was understandable.

'The rest of it's up there.' I said hurriedly. Weighed down by bags, I led the way up the staircase to the heart of my stronghold. Prim stepped up behind me and tapped me on the shoulder. 'Er, Oz. About Mrs Blackstone?'

I frowned. 'I told you, my mother's dead. Anyway, she always bolted the door when she went to the toilet. That was Jan. She does my books, but she sets her own hours.'

Well, it was true. Jan and I were at school together. She did my books. Occasionally she ironed a shirt if she felt sorry for me. On even rarer occasions, when something was troubling her or she just felt like my company, she gave me a cuddle in the night.

Downstairs we heard the toilet flush. I looked across the room. Fortunately my ledgers were spread out on my desk. Prim followed my eyes, then looked around the rest of the place.

31

'You never said it was open plan!'

'You never asked. Anyway, it isn't. The living area's down here. The sleeping area's that raised part, up that wee ladder. When you're in bed, you can't be seen from down here. Well, hardly.'

'Very comforting!' She's good at irony, is Prim.

'Remember the pointy bit I showed you? Well, you get to that through the sleeping area. You see the foot of the second ladder there?'

'It looks sort of like a square funnel from the inside, doesn't it,' she said. At that moment Wallace, the curious iguana, eased his cumbersome frame down the ladder, and swung across to walk along the railing which enclosed the raised area, and against which my bed was pressed.

She shook her head, and then did something which turned my knees to jelly. She stood on her tiptoes and kissed me. Not on the cheek, on the lips. Chastely, you understand. Hands by her side and everything. But still, not on the cheek, on the lips.

'Osbert, you may be a fruitcake, and you may live in a fucking mad-house, but you are my saviour and protector, my knight in shining armour. You're here when I need you, and I thank you.'

The gallows answer stuck in my throat. It was the nicest thing anyone had ever said to me, and I was unspeakably touched.

Jan wasn't. She smiled at Prim as she appeared at the top of the stairs, and she smiled at me. I could grade the warmth of Jan's smiles pretty well, and the one she threw at me was straight from the fridge. She's a tall girl, with looks and dark hair that fell off a Jane Russell poster, and a chest to match.

'Hi,' I said. I was about to add, 'Sorry about surprising you on the bog,' but I thought that I'd better not. 'Jan, this is Prim

32

Phillips. Prim, Jan More. Prim's got a problem, she needs somewhere to crash for a couple of days.'

Jan smiled again, with a glint in her eye, but there was nothing malicious in it. 'Must be a big problem, for you to wind up here. Watch out for Wallace, darlin'. That bloody iguana was right up my kilt this morning.'

She turned back to me. 'Oz, your books are done. Your VAT slip's ready to go. I've written cheques for that and all your other bills, and I've written one for me too.'

'Fine,' I said. I picked up my chequebook, signed the second cheque, tore it out and handed it to her. I didn't even check the amount. Jan hadn't given herself a rise in four years. Mind you, she'd given me a few.

'Thanks. Right, I'm off. See you next month, or whenever.'

I saw her to the door. 'Look, Jan, you'd never believe . . .'

She turned in the doorway, but she was smiling. 'Don't "look" me, Oz. I'd believe anything about you. Our rule is ask no questions, and I'm not going to break it now. Good luck.' She gave my balls a friendly squeeze and closed the door behind her.

I went back upstairs to Prim. She had carried her smaller bag up to the raised area, but had left the monster for me. I looked up and saw her feet disappearing up the ladder to Wallace's sun-room. 'Hey, this is terrific,' her voice echoed down. 'You can see a lot from up here.'

'That's why Wallace likes it,' I shouted back. 'Incidentally, Jan was only kidding about him being up her skirt.' I grabbed the sullen iguana and shoved him into the cage which was his bedchamber, hoping that I was right. The eaves space in the loft was lined with cupboards, where most of my possessions were stored. I dived into one and pulled out a towel. As Prim climbed down the ladder, I threw it to her. 'There. The shower's electric. Instant hot water. You'll find my dressing gown behind the door. Fancy something to eat?'

She thought about it for a few seconds. 'Which takeaway is it at lunchtime? McDonalds?'

I put on a hurt look. 'I do cook sometimes. For example, I do an ace tuna sandwich.'

'That'd be great.' She invaded the vast bag once more and emerged with a bottle of shampoo, and some other stuff. 'Meantime, I have earned this shower. I've come a long way for it. I'm going to enjoy it. Hope your lecky bill can stand it. I may be some time!'

Leaving her to undress, I jumped down to the kitchen. A quick glance at the green things in the bread basket persuaded me that I should take her at her word about lunch. As soon as I heard the bathroom door close, I slipped out of the flat, sprinted down the stairs, out of the building and along the narrow wynd which led to the High Street.

Fortunately there hadn't been a run on Ali's ace tuna, sweetcorn and mayonnaise rolls. I grabbed a handful, added a couple of yoghurts for luck and a quart of milk to replace the yellow stuff in the fridge, and paid my be-turbanned pal. Ali shot me a questioning look, one that said *'Surely not at lunchtime?'* but said nothing. I gave him the expected knowing wink and bolted back the way I had come.

By the time Prim emerged from her shower, I was in my chef's apron, with the woman's naked body turned to the inside and chaste blue stripes on show. Lunch was laid out neatly on plates – the paper bag and wrappers out of sight in the wastebin – and the cafetière was full and steaming. I depressed its plunger with a flourish, and offered her a stool at the breakfast bar, facing mine.

'I'm impressed,' she said. My dressing gown, rarely worn

in any event, had never looked better. It clung to her body, doing things for her that Marks & Spencer could use to great effect in their advertising. My towel looked pretty cool too, wound round her head like an outsize version of my pal Ali's turban. She suited it better than he did.

'Thank you ma'am,' I said. Score a point for the boy.

'I didn't think you were that quick on your feet. I forgot my toothbrush, so I had to run back upstairs. Either you were up in the belvedere or the place was empty.'

'Milk,' I said, assertively. 'Needed some more.'

She bit a huge chunk from a tuna roll. 'Mmm,' she said, as she chewed. 'Pity you didn't get some fresh rolls as well. These are a day or so older than they should be.'

I tried one for myself. 'Nonsense,' I said eventually, relieved to discover that she had been pulling my chain. 'They were fresh this morning.'

We demolished our rolls, slurped our yoghurt and drank our coffee with the enthusiasm of the newly reprieved. Prim held her mug in both hands, leaning forward with her elbows on the bar, holding them carefully so that the dressing gown didn't flop open. I offered her a top-up, but she said, 'No thanks. I really would like an hour or two's kip. I'm not jet-lagged or anything. I was in more or less same time zone. I'm just knackered.'

'Okay, come on and I'll change the bed for you.'

'Er. Oz . . . ?' she said.

'Don't worry about it. The sofa folds down. That's where I sleep when my Dad's here.'

'I'll have that, then.'

'No, because that'll mean I can't work at my desk. I've got a couple of witnesses to interview this afternoon, and I should go back to see Archer.'

The deal was struck. She helped me change the sheets – I'll swear I heard them sigh with relief – making no comment on the stains which were a relic of Jan's last stopover three weeks earlier. As I shook out the Downie, she asked me quietly. 'What are you going to say to Archer?'

I looked at her. 'I could tell him about Kane. If I did that he might decide he had to go to the police. They'd find out what I was really doing there, and that we told them porkies. Then we'd both be in the shit. Your sister would be too, right up to her nose. Alternatively, I could tell him that when I turned up the street was crawling with polis, so I did a runner. That's safer but it leaves us with the problem of what to do about the fiver.'

'Yes,' she said, softly. 'What about the fiver?'

I looked down at her, flexing my sincerity muscles. 'Well,' I said, 'if I hadn't been there you wouldn't have known what the fiver was all about. You might not even have picked it up.'

She shook her head. 'My flat, my fiver. I'd have had it all right.'

'On the other hand, if you hadn't been there to pull that stunt, I'd never have laid a finger on that note. Archer would have had to go public to get it back. So the way I look at it, Miss Primavera Phillips, we're partners.'

She looked at me across the bed. The afternoon sunshine spilled down in a column from the belvedere enveloping her in its light. Slowly, she unwound the towel turban and let it fall to the floor. 'Partners, eh?' she said. Then she reached across the bed and stretched out her hand. It was a chubby wee hand, but her grip was strong. 'Okay, Oz, it's a deal. You know, I didn't come out of the bathroom to get my toothbrush. I came upstairs to fetch the fiver from my jeans pocket. When I found that you were gone but that it was still there, I felt really guilty. You'll do, partner.'

She glanced up; the beam of reflected sunlight glinted off her damp hair and shone in her eyes. 'Let me close the trap door if you're going to sleep,' I said.

'No, leave it. It won't bother me.

'So: will you tell Archer that we've got the note?' she asked.

'I don't know. My gut tells me that the fewer people who know we've got it, the better it'll be for us. You and I have got to face up to some nasty truths about this situation, not least about your sister's part in it. But not now, eh. I've got these people to see, and you've got some kipping to do.'

'Okay.' She was beginning to sound fuzzy. 'One thing though, Oz, partner.'

'What's that?'

'Figure out the best way to tell Archer, but five per cent isn't enough.'

I held up my hands. 'One step at a time. Let's just concentrate on getting through today in one piece. Now sleep!'

I turned and jumped down from the sleeping area. I couldn't help looking back as I hit the lower level, and caught a back view of Prim dropping the dressing gown on the floor and slipping naked into my bed. A quick shudder ran through me from top to toe. I pinched myself hard, but I didn't waken up. If I went back up those steps she'd still be there.

Instead I went across to my desk and began to prepare for my two interviews. Ten minutes later, as I set the telefax to auto answer and picked up my case, soft sleeping sounds floated down from the upper level. She didn't snore; she simply breathed and it was like music whispering its way around the room. I thought of other people who had slept in that bed. My Dad, with his stertorous snores; Jan, with her snorts, snuffles and occasional gentle farts.

Suddenly I had a strange feeling that my loft had been invaded by a haunting spirit, and that life there was never going to be the same again.

In which the Daft Laddie
does a deal.

My two witnesses, coming after my adventures of the morning, were almost refreshingly normal. One was an air steward, who was taking his former employer to an industrial tribunal to contest his dismissal on grounds of sexual misconduct. His defence was that as an adult male over twenty-one he was entitled to have private relations with another man.

The airline's case was that the male staff shower room at Heathrow could not be construed as a private place. I could see that the publicity accruing to my lawyer client would be worth far more than his fee.

My second witness was a punter whose claim for fire damage had been knocked back by his insurance company, and who was suing as a result. The fire had been caused by a faulty gas heater. Neutral though I was, even I could see that his lawyers would have trouble coming up with an answer to the key question. Why had the heater been lit on the afternoon of the hottest day of the year? If the punter's story, 'because

39

my greyhound was sick,' couldn't convince gullible Oz Blackstone, then I could only guess at the likely reaction of the Court of Session.

Archer was waiting for me in his office when I arrived at 4.20 p.m., twenty minutes late. He was almost on tiptoes with tension as he paced around the room.

'Did you see him?'

I still didn't have a clue about what I was going to say to him, so I decided to use the Daft Laddie Gambit as a stalling device. 'See him?' I said, wearing what Granny Blackstone used to call my 'Gowk' expression.

'Willie Kane. Kane and his bird. Did you see them, and have you got the two halves of the fiver?'

Maybe the morning had made me paranoid, but there was something about him, an edge of tension that made me afraid to trust the man. After all, someone had rammed that big knife up under Kane's chin. Someone had searched Prim's flat, and had failed to find the divided banknote. Someone had taken Kane's wallet to hold up the identification of the body.

Suddenly I realised that, if I was to draw up a list of suspects, Mr Raymond Archer would be quite near the top. Nine hundred thousand was a strong lure even to a senior partner, especially if the theft could be blamed on the wee man, and the loss to the firm could be recovered from his assets. Support I had been sent along there just to discover the body, and to fill the time-honoured role of fall guy?

I tried to stop my eyes from narrowing as I looked at him. Playing safe, I decided on Plan B: when cornered, lie with total conviction. I shook my head. 'No. I never got that close. All hell was breaking loose on down there. When I got to Ebeneezer Street, the place was full of blue uniforms, and the entry to the close was guarded. I decided not to announce myself. I didn't even get out the car, just turned it around and drove off.

'I picked up a *News* this afternoon.' I threw the tabloid down on his desk. 'They found a man's body at that address. There's no way of telling which flat it was, but you never know.'

He picked up the paper and scanned the front-page story, which was accompanied by a mugshot of DI Mike Dylan. Either Archer couldn't conceive of Kane being the victim, or he was a bloody good actor.

'What do we do now?' he asked.

'Wait till they identify the body.'

Archer looked at me. 'Surely it couldn't be Willie?'

'Is he immune to knives, then?' I bit my tongue for a second until I remembered that the *News* story, quoting Dylan, had referred to stab wounds.

'But if it is him?'

'Then we have to wait until the police are well clear of the place, then find an excuse to go back in there to try to find the fiver. Unless that's what he was killed for.' That's it Oz boy, plant as many thoughts in his mind as you can, to steer him away from the thought that you might have it. 'Even if it isn't him, we have to let the police get clear before we make contact again.'

Archer thought for a moment. 'Okay. Play it that way. You still happy to work on a contingency basis?' It didn't take me a second to shake my head. 'Not now. It's a new game. I need a fee to cover my time, fifty an hour, plus expenses to Switzerland if we do find the fiver. I want a bigger cut too. Ten per cent's not unreasonable, given the down-side to you if you don't get that money back.'

Archer took even less time to think than I had. 'You're a

41

hard man, Blackstone, but okay. If you pull it off it'll be worth it.' He ushered me to the door. 'Keep in touch.' I was outside in George Street almost before I knew it.

In which secrets are revealed, there is a chance meeting, and deeply held principles are discussed.

Back at the loft, Prim's soft sleeping sounds sounded as if they might go on for a while, but they had been joined by the scrabbling of an irritated iguana. Wallace had his own version of 'Don't fence me in'. He looked at me with a cold imperious eye as I released him.

There were no phone messages, but two faxes from solicitors giving me interview commissions on a non-urgent basis. I switched on my Performa and sat down to type up my notes of the afternoon's interviews. I had almost finished the second, when there was a shout behind me, choked off, followed a few seconds later by a long exhalation.

'Christ, Oz, I was having a dream there about waking up in bed beside that wee man, then I did wake up, beside a bloody lizard!'

'Dinosaur!' I said sternly. I stood up and jumped up on to the sleeping area. Prim was propped up on her right elbow. Her left breast had rolled out over the edge of the Downie, but she hadn't noticed, or didn't care. I sneaked the briefest of glances.

It fulfilled earlier promise, bigger than a handful, but not so large that it was heading rapidly south. I perched myself on the edge of the bed as she sat up, pulling the Downie right under her chin and in the process dislodging Wallace. He shot her a look filled with bale, and reached for the first wooden rung of the ladder to the belvedere.

'Feel better for that?' I asked. I reached out and touched her hand, tentatively. She took mine and gave it a quick squeeze. 'Yes and no,' she said. 'The "yes" part is that you're still the guy I thought you were before I went to sleep, if you know what I mean.' I thought I did, and the hamster who lives in my stomach at such moments did another quick lap of the track. 'What's the "no" bit?' I asked.

'That what happened this morning isn't a movie any more. I have to start treating it as real, and I can't go on blanking Dawn from my mind.'

'Yeah,' I said. 'I know.' I looked at my watch. 'Prim, it's after six. I've got some work to finish off, then I have to get it on the fax. While I do that, why don't you get dressed, then we'll go out somewhere. A drink and a pizza maybe. In the process, partner, we can talk about Dawn, I'll tell you about Archer, and we can decide what we're going to do next.'

She dragged herself along the bed on her bum, until she was right alongside me, the Downie still up to her chin. Then she leaned over and kissed me, on the lips again, and not quite so chastely this time. 'You've just said the magic words, Osbert. I have spent most of the last twelve months dreaming about a drink and a pizza. Now here I am, back home, about to make it all come true, and with a bloke I quite fancy at that.

'I warn you now though: never on the first date, and I mean *never*!'

I didn't know what to say, so she said it for me. 'Sometimes

44

you meet someone and you're attracted right away,' She grinned. 'Like you're attracted to me. So far you're winning: it cuts both ways. Just remember! First date? *Never*!'

I took a hell of a chance. I kissed *her*, on the lips. 'You know the trouble with women?'

'Whssat?'

'You just assume that all us guys are easy lays! I have to go out at least *twice* with a girl before I decide whether she's worthy of my body!'

She dipped her shoulder and shoved me off the bed. 'Go!' she demanded. 'Finish your work, while I turn myself into a human being again.' I did as I was told. Behind me I heard the riffling sound of the Downie being shaken up and spread over the bed. Then Prim's feet sounded lightly on the staircase.

I refocused myself on my reports and finished them off, neat and tidy, set out in question and answer form, with a summary attached. I fed each into the fax then slipped confirmatory copies into envelopes. Quick, experienced and thorough, that's Oz Blackstone, Prince among Private Enquiry Agents, the man most wanted by Edinburgh's legal community, even if much of his work does bore him out of his scone.

I pride myself that on each day of my life I try to learn something new. '*So what's today's lesson, Blackstone?*' I asked myself, out loud, as I stamped the two envelopes.

'**Stick to the boring stuff,**' I answered, '**and forget the Philip Marlowe dreams. Dead people don't look attractive close up, even if the money is good, and the work's exciting.**'

'*That's good, Oz; now what's the bonus lesson?*'

'**That's easy. Don't give up believing in miracles. Most people find at least one in a lifetime.**'

I turned around, and there she was, Primavera, Springtime in Spanish, standing beside the bed, fastening a single string of pearls around her neck. The jeans and tee-shirt had gone, to be replaced by a close-fitting grey skirt and a sleeveless white blouse. Her sun-bleached hair had been teased into order, carefully but casually, and she was made up with blue eye shadow, a touch of blusher and a vivid red lipstick which sat on her perfect mouth like country wine on a summer evening. She was so beautiful that she made me breathless.

I stood there, dumbstruck for a while, until the inevitable nonsense sprang to my tongue. 'Springtime,' I said, holding out a hand in invitation, 'would you care to join me in my garden?'

My loft opens out on to a tiny terrace, on which a few geraniums and a woebegone palm struggle for survival in the heart of my Scottish city. I threw open the double doors, and held out my hand for her as she approached across the big room, passing through a beam of light from one of the four Vellux windows set on each side of the sloping ceiling.

If I was an aesthete I would say that sunlit May evenings are my favourite time of the year in Edinburgh. Those few days, as the year shakes off the dying grip of winter, can be sublime. They are moments not to be missed, yet all too fleeting, before the Scottish summer asserts itself in all its wet, windy drabness.

As Prim stepped out on to my south-facing terrace, I felt suddenly full up, and it came to me that this was one of those times in my life that I'll remember on my dying day.

My fifth birthday, when my Mum baked a cake, I had a party, and my Dad gave me my first set of real football boots. My first day at primary school. My first Hearts–Hibs game. My first day at secondary school. Sneaking in among my sister's crowd one night to watch a bootleg video of *The Exorcist*, and being chucked out for laughing at the bit where Linda Blair's head spins all the way round. My first, and last, cigarette. My first fumbling, incompetent but affectionate shag with Jan at a party in her house while her folks were away. My Mother's death. A weekend my Dad and I spent walking in Derbyshire, eating wholesome food and drinking a different beer every night, as part of his emergence from our bereavement.

Seminal moments all of them; now here she was, this woman I had met in the most bizarre circumstances a few hours earlier, taking her place, perhaps at the head of them all.

She looked out across the southern aspect of Edinburgh, across Arthur's Seat, up the ragged line of the Old Town's rooftops, up to the craggy Castle on its flat-topped hill. She breathed deeply of the evening air. She took my arm, and squeezing it, leaned against me, laying her head on my shoulder. 'It's good to be back, partner,' she said, softly and musically. 'If only for now.'

There was nothing I could say to add to the moment, and so, for once in my life, I said nothing. Instead, I eased her gently into one of the two green wooden folding chairs on the balcony. I stepped back into the house and trotted down to the kitchen, re-emerging from the loft a couple of minutes later with two glasses and my prize bottle of reasonably good champagne. It had been a present from a lawyer client, and had been languishing in my fridge since Christmas, awaiting an appropriate moment. I balanced the glass on the balcony's broad wooden rail and filled them carefully. Handing one to Prim I raised the other in a toast. 'You're back; so welcome,' I said. 'I hope that it's for good.'

She looked at me for a long time, the glass pressed to her

lips. 'We'll see,' she said at last. 'When I left a year ago, it was because I didn't have anything to stay for. For now though, as I say, I'm glad I'm back.' She sipped the champagne and nodded in polite approval. We drank in silence, looking out over the park, watching the joggers on the Radical Road, until the sun slipped round the corner of the loft, and the balcony, and my shivering palm tree, fell into shade.

'Come on,' I said. 'Let's go on a pizza hunt. D'you fancy a walk first? Along Princes Street?' She nodded. I left her outside for a minute or two while I changed into my pub-going gear, then, locking up everything but Wallace's cage, we headed out and up towards the old High Street. 'You got that fiver?' I asked as we left.

'Too damn right!'

'Well look after it. Don't spend it, or anything daft like that.'

She gave me a woman's smile which made it clear that there was no chance of that happening.

It was Thursday, and so, although it was evening, the city was bustling with shoppers. We walked arm-in-arm, up towards St Giles, turning on to the Mound and down the long flight of steps which led down to the National Gallery and to Princes Street beyond. The pavement outside the record shops and bookstores towards the West End was thick with people and so we turned up Castle Street and along Rose Street, until it opened out into Charlotte Square.

'Drink first?'

She nodded. 'I could slaughter a pint.' '*Oh Jesus*,' I thought, '*this woman gets better and better*!'

We walked along the square's south side and down the few steps to Whigham's. As usual it was thronged. I excused my way up to the high counter and ordered a pint of lager for the lady, bartender if you please, and the same of the day's guest beer, Old Throgmorton's Embalming Fluid or something similar, for me. We found elbow space at a shelf beside the bar. Prim closed her eyes and took a deep swallow. 'Not the same as champagne, but not too damn bad either,' she said. 'Okay, Osbert. Out with it. Tell me about your life.'

I jammed my knuckles against my forehead. 'Where shall I begin?

'It's pretty dull really. I'm twenty-nine years old, staring the big Three-Oh in the face. I was born in Cupar. My Dad's a dentist and my Mum was a teacher, so I'm a real middle-class boy. When I was four, we moved to Anstruther, and my Dad lives there still. I meant it about my Mother being dead. That happened nine years ago. Dad was doing her teeth one Saturday morning, and he took an X-ray. He found a shadow on her jawbone. From being perfectly well that day, she was gone in seven months.' I tried to tell her that part of the story as casually as I could, but that's a trick I've never mastered. I tried to hide it with a swallow of Old Throgmorton's, but Prim saw through me. She touched my cheek, lightly. 'Poor thing,' she said.

'Who? Me or my Mum?'

'All of you. It must have been dreadful for your Dad.'

'Yeah, it was. He was chewed up with guilt. He saw her through to the end, and then he started on a course of serious therapeutic drinking. He'd always liked a bevvy – as I said, he's a dentist – but this was something he was doing as a punishment. Ellen was at home at the time, I was at university. Eventually she called me about it.

'I went up to Anstruther for a weekend, and watched him at it. He did his regular Saturday morning surgery, as usual, then started into the Bacardi and Coke for lunch. After a while I sat him down at the table and I said, 'For fuck's sake, Dad, this has got to stop. That Coke is *murder* on the teeth.' He looked at me and he laughed. Then he began to cry. He cried all day, and all through Sunday. Monday was a holiday, so he and I played golf. Then we went to the cemetery and said hello to Mum. We both sensed the same thing, that she was pleased to see us. He was all right after that. We visit each other a lot now. He comes down here, I go up to Anstruther. He sees a bit of Jan's mother. She teaches in the same school my Mum did. She's divorced and they live near each other.

'Ellen's my sister, by the way. She's three years older than me. She's nice, our Ellen, but she's married to a real chuckie. He's in Marketing with an oil company. They moved out to France last year. He works in Lyon, and they live a bit outside it, quite close to the Swiss border. It's funny, when we were kids I thought Ellen was a real tough cookie. No, scratch that, Ellen *was* a real tough cookie. Now she's a housewife, with a teaching qualification and no job, waiting on her man and, as far as I can gather being ignored by him most of the time.'

I looked at her. 'Bored?'

'No, fascinated. Go on.'

I sloshed some more of the old T down my neck. 'Where was I? Grew up in Anstruther, played for the school team, kept myself physically intact by being the fastest thing on two feet in the whole school. Buggery was a playground sport in our place, but none of the guys with low foreheads and trailing knuckles could catch me!

'I left school at eighteen and came to Edinburgh to do an Arts degree. I've been here ever since. I came out with a two—two in Philosophy, Politics and Economics. I had dreams of getting a job as a researcher for the Labour Party, but I discovered that those jobs were filled by firsts or two—ones, and more often than not by Americans. I also discovered that my Mum's death had left me feeling that politics isn't worth a monkey's anyway. So I joined the police.

'I hated it from Day One, but after I'd been in a few months, I met a pal from university. He was working for an Investigation Agency, and he said that they'd a vacancy. So I hung up my truncheon and went to work for them.'

'I thought you were self-employed?'

I tilted my head back and sent the last of the Old Throggies on the start of the long journey to the sea. 'I am. The guys we worked for were a pair of real rat bastards. They were ex-RAF Military Policemen, and they'd taken their talents for persecution into the private sector. They came from the time when there were big bucks to be made from matrimonial work, and they were never happier than when they were photographing a misbehaving couple on the job, or pounding on hotel room doors, shouting "Come out, come out, the game's a bogey!" I could see that these plonkers were living in the past, and I couldn't see why they should be doing so on the strength of our honest toil.

'So I hung in there for a year, until the clients got to know me. Then my pal Jimmy and I went round them all, offered them the same service for less money than Fagin and Bill Sykes were charging, and signed the lot up. We ran it as a partnership until three years ago, when Jimmy's Dad retired and he went off to run his pub. Since then I've been on my own, although Jimmy still helps me out when I'm on holiday, or over-booked.

'When I'm not working, I play golf with my Dad, go to the movies, listen to an eclectic collection of music, and pursue women.'

'You mean they don't pursue you?'

51

She finished her lager. 'Two for the road?' she asked, gladdening my heart still more. A woman who buys her round! I nodded, and she eased her way through to the bar, fishing a tenner from her purse as she went. I watched, anxiously, to make sure that not even one half of the fiver slipped out.

She was back in a couple of minutes, carrying a pint in each hand. 'On the subject of women . . .' she began. I guessed what was coming. '. . . what about Jan? If your Dad and her Mum are friends, how about you two?'

'Jan's great. We grew up together. Same class at school and all that. She's someone's dream woman, no doubt about it, but not mine. We tried the getting serious bit, went on holiday together a couple of times, but we agreed early on it wouldn't work long-term. We know that we're best off being pals. I haven't had a real steady since Thingummy left a few years back. Jan, on the other hand, if she felt like it, could pull blokes as easy as picking her nose. She's just got her own tastes, that's all.'

She looked at me over the top of her glass, teasing. 'And you haven't?'

For once I was ready. 'Oh contrayre, Madame. Fussiest of the fussy, that's Oz Blackstone. Look at the company I keep.'

She smiled, and I wasn't sure that under the blusher, she wasn't blushing. I slipped my arms around her waist and drew her against me. We smiled at each other, saying nothing, but exchanging secrets and making promises for the not-too-distant future. Yet I could tell that underneath it all her sexual self-confidence was something of an act. Every so often she would break off eye contact, only to look up again into my face, with a half-grin that said, 'Be kind to me, that's all I ask.'

'Of course I will,' I said, and she understood. I felt the air begin to sizzle between us. '*It's kissing time in Whighams,*' I thought. We leaned closer to each other.

'Hey there, you two!' The voice was unmistakable. We separated and looked across the crowded bar, guiltily I expect, at the gallus figure of Mike Dylan. As he pushed his way over to us, another man followed behind him. Dylan's introduction was unnecessary; I knew this one well enough. He even knew me. 'This is my boss,' said Dylan, 'Detective Superintendent Richard Ross, area head of CID. I was just filling him in on this morning's events.

'These are the poor people who found the body. Miss Phillips and Mr Blackstone.' He looked at me, with just a trace of truculence. I could read his mind. '*Tough shit, Dylan,*' I wanted to say, '*she's taken.*'

Ricky Ross was a different sort of copper to the DI. For a start he really *was* a Clever Bastard. He was a big, athletic bloke, good-looking, his dark hair flecked with grey; a man of substance in every way, unlike his sidekick, who had nothing behind the Armani suit but brass neck and ambition. In his younger days, he'd been quite a sportsman, with about a dozen rugby caps for Scotland as a flank forward. 'I remember you,' he said. 'Oxgangs, a few years back. You were a probationer, but you took our training into the PI line. I forgave you, though, when you stitched up those two bastards Banks and McHugh. They needed taking care of. So how's business?'

I gave him the obligatory shrug. 'I'm doing all right. Not as well as you, though. You seem never to be out of the bloody papers.'

It was his turn to shrug. 'People keep committing crimes, we keep clearing them up. It's the law of supply and demand in reverse. The public demands action, my lot supply it, and I take the credit.'

He glanced at me with a grin I didn't like. 'You must have

had a scare this morning. Christ, I remember you on a turn-out once. It was a drugs overdose, but CID got involved. You were the greenest probationer I'd ever seen, greener even than Michael here at his first murder.'

He looked down at Prim. 'And how about you, Miss Phillips? Are you okay now?'

'Fine thanks,' said Prim. 'I'm just glad that Oz was with me, otherwise I'd have been scared to death.'

'Mmm,' said Ross, with a half-smile. 'Just as well. Tell me, have you made contact with your sister yet?'

She looked up at him, sharply. 'I haven't a clue where my sister is, any more than I know which of her friends had the key to my flat. Believe me, when I find out . . .'

Ross nodded. 'Aye, sure. Just let us know when you do.'

I decided to chance my arm. 'Have you identified the body yet?'

'Naw,' said Ross. 'Not a notion. We were thinking about circulating a description of his cock. That's probably our best chance of a response.'

Prim frowned at him. She has a rare talent for making men feel ill at ease, but Ricky Ross was beyond her reach. He simply ignored her, continuing to smile at me. 'Nae use to him now though, Blackstone, is it? Wonder if he's left it to anyone in his will?'

'Aye,' I agreed, 'and even if it was shared out, I can think of a couple of polismen who'd find just half of it an improvement! Present company excepted, of course,' I added, after a pause. 'Can I get you a drink?' I asked, as Prim spluttered beside me.

The phrase 'Can I get you a drink?' is a device which is, as far as I know, peculiar to Edinburgh. Its meaning depends entirely on the company in which the enquirer finds himself, and, with the finest inflection, shifts from a wholly sincere, 'Can I get you a drink?' to an equally sincere, 'If that's all you've got to say, why don't you fuck off and leave us alone?'

Ross read my meaning correctly. 'No thanks, we're meeting someone. He's over there, in fact.' I turned to follow his gaze and caught the eye of a thin, sallow man, who I seemed to remember was a car dealer with a reputation for supplying MOT's to fit all price ranges.

'Oh. Okay, then. We'll look in tomorrow to give you those statements, Inspector.'

The men in suits made their way round the bar, the pack opening up to let them pass at my deliberately loud mention of Dylan's rank. As they reached the other side, Ricky Ross shot a look towards us, back across the crowded room, which made me feel suddenly that I might just have taken too big a liberty.

'I didn't like him at all!' said Prim, as they were out of earshot.

'No,' I said. 'Welcome to the club. It's difficult to underestimate a bloke like Dylan, but Ross is in a different league. He operates at a much higher level of nastiness.'

I reached for my glass, but found that during our conversation with the forces of the law an over-zealous bar steward, or an out and out thief, had removed it, and Prim's lager, although each had been at least half-full. I started towards the bar, but she tugged my arm. 'Come on. Forget those, it's time for that pizza.'

I should have known. It was Thursday and so the Bar Roma was heaving, without a table in sight. Prim looked at me, frustrated beyond belief, until I put yet another Plan B into operation. We commandeered a taxi from the rank outside Fraser's and headed for the Pizzarama, halfway up Leith Walk, purveyors of the biggest pizza in town. We bought two monsters to go, then grabbed another taxi and went back to the loft and my extensive, if inexpensive, wine cellar.

A great takeaway pizza is always slightly underdone. The Pizzarama giants, covered in tomato, pepperoni, ham, artichokes and God knew what else, fitted into my oven at a squeeze, and by the time we had finished the champagne – if you leave a teaspoon in the neck of an opened bottle of fizz, it keeps its fizziness; not many people know that – and opened a bottle of Safeway Chianti, they were ready.

Watching Prim eat her first pizza for a year was another of those seminal whatnots. She cut the huge thing into segments which she attacked with her fingers, savouring each ripped-off mouthful, smiling all the time, even as she chewed. When she finished, I still had a third of mine to go. She looked across the breakfast bar at me, her eyes huge and appealing. 'Okay,' I said. 'I give in. Would you like some more, my dear?'

The Chianti was new and strong. As we reached the end of the bottle, I felt relaxed, uninhibited and very, very . . .

Prim licked the last of the pizza from her fingers and gazed across at me. 'Remember that poor young policeman today?'

'Who could forget the poor wee bugger? And that effing troll stood in the doorway trying not to hear him? Why d'you ask?'

'It's just that tonight, when you said what you said to Ross, I thought for a second, I was going to do the same thing as the boy did.'

'I'm almost sorry you didn't. There have been many firsts in my life today. That would have been yet another.'

She drained her glass, and reached for another bottle from the rack, but I reached out a hand and stopped her.

'Prim,' I said, doing my level best to make my eyes outshine anything in the night sky, framed in the kitchen window. 'I've been thinking. How would it be – and this has to be a mutually agreed thing, you understand – if we decided, first of all that our deeply held principles and rules must remain unbroken, but that in all the circumstances, you should regard lunch today as having been our first date, and by the same token, that should regard myself as having been out with you at least twice?'

Our elbows were on the breakfast bar. I slipped my right hand into hers, as if we were about to arm-wrestle, and pulled her gently towards me. I kissed her, on the lips again, on her full red lips, not at all chastely this time. Her mouth opened, and I felt her tongue flick against my teeth.

She tasted of the finest sweet wine, delicious, refreshing, making me long for more.

'In all the circumstances,' she whispered, our foreheads touching lightly, 'and given the duration of our acquaintance I would say that such an agreement is, at this moment in time, absolutely . . .'

In which the Earth moves.

'**P**rimavera, Primavera . . .' I moaned her name in the moonlight which flooded down upon us from the belvedere. She leaned over me, kissing my chest, gently biting my nipples, responding to my touch and moving her self against my hands.

'Where have you come from?' I asked, drawing her down upon me, and throwing the quilt to one side so that I could wallow again in the perfection of her body, in her firm, full, big-nippled breasts, in the amazing narrowness of her waist, in the round curve of her hips, in the flatness of her belly, in the thick nest of wiry blonde hair at her centre, shining and sparkling as she moved in the moonbeam.

'I've always been here,' she said, and she kissed me with her lips of velvet, as I had never been kissed before. 'I think we've both been moving towards each other, all our lives. I believe in destiny. You're part of mine, I'm part of yours. We were set on a course towards each other.'

'And will we go on together, Springtime and Oz?'

'Who knows? That's the thing about destiny; you believe in it and let it take you where it will. *Right now* we're together, and it's always the now that counts.'

I rolled over with Springtime in my arms, burying my face in her. As I flicked my tongue in and out of her navel, she gasped and arched her back. 'I want you now. I need you now. Come into me now.'

I placed a finger across her lips. 'Time enough,' I said, although she could see that I was more than ready. I bent and kissed the inside of her thighs as she spread them wide, licking my way towards her. She moaned again. 'Now, Oz, now.'

'Yes, Primavera, yes!' I covered her and she took me into herself with a supple movement, the sweetest embrace I had ever known. We lay entwined, barely moving. Her tongue was in my mouth again, her fingers wound through my crinkly hair. She pulled my head back and looked at me with smouldering eyes. 'This is right!' she hissed. Then her eyelids flickered and she began to shudder, gripping me tight, inside, tighter than I had ever imagined. Her fingers dug into my back, and she cried out, once, twice, again, again. And then I realised that two voices were calling out and that one of them was mine. I was lost. As I thrust into her and held myself there, we were washed by wave upon wave of sensation, by a feeling that every nerve-ending in our bodies was being bathed in soothing oil. It went on and on until I thought it would never stop, but finally the crest was reached and we started back down the slope towards the world, a world which I knew now, for certain, would never be the same again.

She lay there, eyes closed, with a sheen of sweat on her face. I licked it off; she tasted salty and sublime on my tongue. I felt myself start to subside, but she held me inside her. 'No, don't go,' she sighed. 'I want to keep you there for ever.'

'That's all right with me,' I said. 'I can't think of a better place to be. Primavera . . . stop me if you think I'm being daft, but . . . Primavera Phillips, you are the most beautiful, wonderful woman I have ever met, and I love you. You're the dream I've had all my life, and now you're here.

'I know we've still to see our first sun come up together, but say you'll stay with me.'

She touched my cheek with her soft, strong hand. 'I'll stay with you for now, Osbert Blackstone. But you're crazy; you don't know me. You never really know another person. Some people, many people, maybe most people don't even know themselves.'

I smiled, filled up to the brim with more happiness than I had ever imagined I could hold. '*I* know myself, lover. And whatever you say I know you too. I want you now, and for all the tomorrows I've got coming.'

We lay there, in each other's arms, together. I closed my eyes, as she began to move over my body, sliding, animalistic. Suddenly I felt her nails dig deep into my chest. I don't mind being submissive on the odd occasion, but I've never been too good at masochism.

'Oww!' I yelled with the pain . . .

. . . and suddenly I was wide awake, staring into Wallace's accusatory reptilian eye. His claws were digging sharply into my pecs as he balanced himself upon me.

'Get off me, you green bastard,' I hissed, picking him up, carefully to avoid ripping more flesh, and placing him gently on the floor. I had forgotten that the settee was one of Wallace's favourite night-spots. I lay there, under my lonely blanket, in my bulging boxers, and tried to go back to my dream. But it was no use. Instead, I lay there, listening to the sleep sounds of Primavera Phillips, comparing them with

61

those of Jan, my other night visitor. I decided that they were much the same, except that I hadn't noticed Prim farting yet.

'Two people are truly together,' my Dad told me once, when he was giving me my degree course in the meaning of life, 'only when they can fart freely and as loud as they please in each other's company.' I remember looking at him, appalled, quite certain that my Mother had never farted in her life.

I chuckled in the dark, quietly, lest I disturb Prim's melodious sleep.

'. . . at this moment in time, absolutely out of the question.' She had said, but with a delicious smile that told me she was in no way offended that I had put the proposition to her. And so we had retired, she to the bed, and me to the instrument called my sofa-bed. I can never decide whether it is an instrument of torture or of music. Some nights it's both as your toes and knuckles hit the sharp-cornered metal frame or as the springs dig into you, singing out tunelessly as you twist and turn, trying to negotiate the pathway to sleep's dark gate.

I rolled over on to my side and the full spring orchestra played. The twang even startled Wallace. I heard Prim start from her sleep, and saw her silhouette as she sat up.

'Sorry,' I said. 'This thing can be bloody noisy.' I bounced on the machine to show what had wakened her. 'I'll try to lie still.'

'No, it's okay. I had a good kip during the day, remember. What time is it?'

'Around five, I think.'

'Ow. D'you want to swop over? You take the bed and I'll have the sofa?'

'Thanks, but it's okay,' I said to her. I paused. 'Hey, now we're awake how about you telling me your life story. Let me into all your secrets. After that, how would it be if we get up and go for a walk up Arthur's Seat, to watch the sun come up behind Berwick Law?'

There was silence as she weighed my latest proposition. 'Yes,' she said at last. 'You know, Oz, my love . . .' Her tone may have been bantering, but my heart jumped as she said the word. '. . . I reckon that if I stripped everything away from you, right at your core I'd find a hopeless romantic . . . just like me. Yes, let's go for that walk.

'But first, the unexpurgated adventures of Primavera Phillips. If you think you're ready.'

Twenty minutes later, there was nothing I didn't know about her. She had been born in Auchterarder to her oddball parents thirty years before. Her mother – when she wasn't reading Barbara Taylor Bradford – had been a social worker, but was now a moderately successful writer of children's books. Her father's modelmaking had evolved from a cabinetmaking and furniture design business. She and her sister Dawn, who was five years younger, had been educated solidly at local authority schools, until they had been old enough to escape from their home village.

Prim had trained as a nurse in Glasgow, and had worked in Edinburgh Royal, before joining the dedicated staff of St Columba's Hospice. 'If you'd been there a few years earlier, you'd have nursed my Mum,' I said, when she told me. 'That's a vocation, and no mistake.'

'Yes, I thought it was, but it wore off after four years. I found that was I drinking too much; worse than that, I was drinking too much on my own, at home. I was narky, too, all the time. I wasn't me, any more.' I sensed her looking at me in the dark, suddenly, strangely intense. 'Never forget that, Oz. I always have to be me!'

In the gloom, I could see her scratching her nose. 'I don't

know why, but while I was working there, gradually I gave up men. Not that I was promiscuous, mind you. Up until now, I've had six lovers, but hospice work turned me into a celibate.'

I propped myself upon an elbow. 'What are the chances of a miracle cure?'

'Let's just put it this way,' she said, with a laugh in her husky voice. 'A vacancy may arise in the future. Your application for the post has been noted, and is under consideration. You will be advised of the outcome in due course. For now, that's all I'm saying.'

I tried to look solemn. 'Thank you for that information. You may keep my application and my CV on your files until further notice.' I've never been much good at solemnity. I grinned in the dark. 'So when did you notice the first signs of a thaw?'

'This afternoon. When I woke up in your bed with that weird bloody iguana alongside me! I looked across at you, and saw you at work, and I thought *"Look at that daft bugger there! What's he like?"* And all of a sudden I felt that, yes, it might be possible to get some fun out of life again.'

I almost said, 'Oh it is! Let me show you!' Instead, trying to convince her that I really am responsible and self-disciplined, I steered the conversation back on course.

'Why did you leave the hospice? Had you just had enough?'

'Yeah; as much as I could take. One thing more than any other finished me, though; I had this pal on the staff. She hit the compassion wall, and left. A year later, she was back as a patient. We couldn't tell her anything about what was happening, of course. She knew it all. The day she died, I resigned, to give myself a chance to forget. I never will though. I'll never go far enough to forget that.'

'Is that why you went to Africa? To forget?'

'No. I had reasons, two of them. First, I was overcome by a sudden inability to sit still. It didn't matter where I was, I felt shut in. Second, I wanted to help people live, not die. I got very grand, and decided to go on a personal crusade. So I answered an ad, and went to work for a UN-sponsored agency in Central Africa. I thought I'd be teaching nutrition, working with babies, that sort of thing. So I was, for two months. Then a Civil War started, and the casualties started to arrive.

'I had no idea what modern armaments can do to the human body. Now I have. I've patched them up, and helped cut bits off. But there's worse; you have no idea what people can do to other people. That wee man yesterday, he had a quick finish, believe me. The story I told Dylan was true, but . . .' Even in the night, I could see her shudder, suddenly, '. . . what they did to the women!'

'Was it like that for a whole year?'

'No, I couldn't have taken that. We were rotated. Most of the time we were in a hospital in a safe zone, but every so often we were asked to go up front with the troops.'

Now it was my turn to shudder. 'Weren't you in danger?'

'I don't think so. We had UN soldiers as our escort. They taught us to shoot, too, and gave us handguns.'

'Christ, I must remember that!'

'You do that! I'm a crack shot.'

'Me too,' I murmured, too quietly for her to hear.

In which the Earth moves . . . again.

Back to back like old school chums, we dressed ourselves in heavy sweaters, jeans and boots . . . Primavera seemed to have everything in that vast holdall.

I drove us down Holyrood Road and into the Queen's Park, up the hill to the wee loch, where, thanks to the trippers, no ducks ever had it so good. The moon was long gone, but there was a hint of daybreak in the east as we set off up the steep slopes of Arthur's seat, so that we could see the path well enough. Prim took the lead; gallantly, I thought, I allowed her to go ahead. It took me around three minutes to realise that she had mountain goat in her ancestry. Our conversation dried up as I saved my breath to keep up with her brisk pace. Up and up we climbed, scrambling hand and foot up the final stretch, until we came to the summit of the old volcano, to stand beside the Solstice cairn.

At our backs, the street lights of the Old Town shone softly, and the floodlit buildings stood out on the hill, with the Castle at its summit. Before us, as we looked east, recovering our breath, the day was beginning to assert itself. Around twenty miles away, we could see the outline of North Berwick Law, a slightly scaled-down version of the hill on which we stood. All down the Forth, in the mouth of the estuary, lighthouses still sent out their signature beams; on the great seagull's head that was the Bass Rock, away across at Barns Ness in Fife and most distant of all on the Island of May.

I took out two Mars bars which I had secreted about my person, and handed one to my lady. 'There y'are, Springtime. Our first breakfast together!'

She looked and laughed, 'Did you make these at the same time you made those tuna rolls yesterday?'

'Aye. I'm a dab hand. They're not a patch on my Curlywurly though!' See me, see sexual innuendo!

We looked eastward again and saw the line of light along the horizon deepen, and eat its way upward into the sky, diluting and beating back the darkness. Patches of morning mist lay in gullies along the plain between the Lammermuir Hills and the sea, moving and shifting very slowly, as they began to yield to the rising temperature.

'It's like being in an aeroplane, above the clouds,' said Prim. 'Do you do this often?'

I looked down at her, held in the circle of my arm, and I smiled. 'Never done it in my life before. It's been one of those things you think of doing, but never quite get round to. Tonight, this morning, whatever, I realise that I've been saving it to share with the right person.'

'That's very profound, for you, Osbert.'

'Aye, but don't worry, I'll be back to normal soon.'

Around the Law, in the distance, the light began to intensify. We watched as it strengthened; we watched the rotation of the planet at the horizon dipped, revealing the great golden ball, and the day began. 'D'you realise what's happening, Primavera? The Earth's moving for us!'

She squeezed me tight, almost crushing my ribs. 'I was right, Blackstone. You're a romantic to the core.' She stood up on tiptoe and she kissed me, softly, her arms round my neck, my arms encircling her narrow waist. 'D'you still fancy me, then, even in this gear?' she asked.

'Dressed from head to toe in a black bin-liner, I'd still fancy you,' I said in a sudden outburst of total candour. Something welled up in my throat, and I realised it was a lump.

Suddenly there was a noise below us, a panting, scrambling noise. We looked down in surprise, to see the first of the morning joggers cresting the summit. She pulled herself on to the small flat peak and fell face-first against the cairn, gasping.

'Morning,' said I.

The woman looked round. 'Christ, you're early,' she spluttered.

'Oh, I'm sorry to disappoint you, Miss,' I said. 'I'm not him. He's got a beard, and he wears a dress. You never know though, if you wait long enough, this is the sort of place where he might turn up. More likely it'll be in Glasgow, though. He's more needed there.

'Come Magdalene,' I said, tugging Prim's waist, and wincing as she nipped my bum to shut me up. 'We'd best get back down.

'So long,' I said to the speechless, knackered jogger. 'Enjoy the morning, it's worth the effort.'

We picked our way down the almost sheer path from the summit, on to the gentler, but still steep descent. Two more runners were starting out from the road below. As we walked hand in hand, more relaxed than on the ascent, a flight of swans made their way slowly and clumsily across the sky, on their way to St Margaret's Loch and another hard day's work, posing for tourist photographers and gobbling stale breadcrumbs.

'They're not very good at flying, are they,' said Prim.

'Thank the Lord for that. They're good in the water and aggressive on land. If they were air aces as well the CIA would be training them as operatives!'

As we walked on down the path, a piece of the day before came back into my mind. 'Prim, that bottle in the kitchen. Prozac. Why should Dawn be on the happy pills?'

She looked up at me anxiously. 'I don't know. It came as a shock to me. Dawn's always been moody, very up one minute, very down the next. Maybe, with me being away, there's been no-one to help her through the down bits.'

'Not even Willie Kane?'

'Seems not.'

There were three more parked cars when we reached the roadway, one per jogger, I assumed. We drove around the south side of the great hill, until the Old Town stretched before us again, blinking itself awake. I parked and we walked up to the High Street, to pick up the makings of a real breakfast from Ali's.

The turbanned one was on duty early as always. If there are people there and pennies to be taken in, Ali will take them. 'Hullaw ther, Ozzie,' he bellowed. I've never been quite sure whether Ali accentuates his Scots accent. 'Hullaw tae you, hen,' he added, catching sight of Prim.

'Ali, this is Miss Phillips. Remember her and don't give her any of your past sell-by stuff.

'See him, love,' I said, pointing to the grinning Asiatic. 'This one is Edinburgh's cheekiest grocer. Ali thinks customer relations means . . . No. On second thoughts I don't think I'll tell you that!'

Ali's one of my best pals. He and I, and eight other nutters, play five-a-side football together at Meadowbank Stadium, every Tuesday evening in life. We arrange our lives around our weekly session, which, like most informal football clubs, is simply on excuse for a few bevvies.

Ali's at his best as a defender. Me, I see myself as a cultured midfielder, in the Jim Baxter mould. The truth is, the Great Jim and I have one thing in common. We're both Fifers; that's it. Where he could have opened a combination lock with his left foot, mine is purely for standing on. The other one isn't up to much either, except that in our team, I am the acknowledged master of the toe-poke, a distinctive way of shooting, stiff-ankled, with great power and accuracy. The toe-poke is derided by all serious footballers, and brings me much scorn, but usually from opponents, as they pick the ball out of their net.

That morning, instead of a neat through ball, Ali passed me bacon, eggs, rolls, bread, orange juice, honey, milk and, on a 'Please,' from Primavera, square, spicy, sliced Lorne sausage. Continentals look down on the British as sausage-makers. Their idea of sausage is something to be sliced razor thin, something that looks as if it came out of an animal, rather than being made from it. Give me German, French, Italian or Spaniard, and let me confront any one with a square slice of Ali's Scottish sausage, grilled, in a white crusty roll. That would put the buggers in their place.

We ate ours with HP sauce for extra body, washing them down with orange juice. Then we showered and dressed for the day. I suggested showering together to save energy, but Prim offered me a pound coin for the meter.

Afterwards, we sat upstairs on the sofa in the loft, Primavera in my dressing gown and me in a sort of towelling kilt thing with a Velcro fastening that an ex had given me one Christmas and which I found buried in a heap at the foot of the wardrobe. The doors were open, and Wallace lay somnolent on the terrace, looking back at us, occasionally and disdainfully. Wallace lives for three things, sunshine, sleep and sustenance. The last of these takes many forms, most of them crunchy.

On our first morning together we drank honey-sweetened tea, settling into our new situation. I punched her shoulder lightly. 'Hey, Springtime. If I get that job we were talking about how about bringing the rest of your stuff down here?'

She looked at me, seriously for once, just a bit guarded. My stomach twitched.

'It's fine where it is just now. First things first. I've been putting off the evil hour, but I've got to find out what's happened to my sister.

'I don't believe for a second that Dawn killed that poor wee man; but she *has* disappeared. Before we think about what we do with that fiver, I've got to know where Dawn is, and to be sure she's all right. Oz, you're the detective. I need your help.'

I squeezed her hand. 'I told you love, I'm an enquiry agent, not a private eye. Different jobs, different people. But for you and Dawn, I'll help all I can.'

I sat silent for a while, trying to think not just about facts, but about the conclusions which they suggest. All my working life, I've trained myself not to use my imagination, or to encourage in any way embroidery by witnesses. All of a sudden I found that putting my mind to work, as well as my listening, interviewing and literacy skills, was a stimulating prospect.

'Okay then. What we have to do is to think of the options, and discount them if we can.

'One, and let me finish. Are you wrong, and *did* Dawn bump off Mighty Mouse? Did she encourage him to embezzle the money, and set up the bank account, with the intention of killing him when the time came?' Prim frowned at me, and shook her head.

'Think of how we found Kane. He died having sex, or at the very least in an aroused state. The police lab will know by now which it was. Whichever, he was Dawn's lover, so that seems to put her at the scene. Did she get him excited, get on top of him and at the right moment produce that knife from under the bedclothes and summon up the strength to shove it up under his chin? That's Option One.'

'And I don't believe it, not for one bloody minute!' said Prim, vehemently.

I shrugged my shoulders. 'I don't either, but it's the easy option, and that's the one the police will go for, unless we can show them different.

'Option Two. Dawn has another man, an accomplice. They found Kane, set him up by the oldest means known to mankind, then the other bloke killed him. That paints a nasty picture, and I don't buy that either, but again, when they know the whole story, the police would. They could even find a second suspect without too much trouble.'

She looked at me, puzzled. 'Who?'

'Raymond Archer. He knew everything about that firm. He could have done everything that he told me Kane did, if he'd had Dawn to help him. Sending me along to find the body could just have been part of it.'

'Okay,' said Primavera. 'So what's Option Three?'

'Someone else knows about the fraud, and about the bank account. He breaks into the flat, and kills Kane. He tried to make Dawn give him the fiver, but she persuades him she doesn't know where it is. He leaves and takes her with him.

'Again, that someone else could just be Archer.'

I squeezed her hand again and turned her face towards me. 'Those are all the possibilities I can see. I prefer the third one, for a very good reason. If either one or two was right, the banknote wouldn't still have been there for the police to find and you to pick up. My best guess is that Dawn's been taken, and that she's safe. Without her, the guy has a slim chance of getting his hands on that fiver.'

She looked me in the eye, earnestly. 'Thanks Oz, but there is a fourth choice. Maybe Dawn wasn't there at all. Maybe the story I spun the police was true. Maybe it was someone else.'

'Yes, Prim, and maybe Willie Kane, the poor, innocent, browbeaten, middle-aged, infatuated stockbroker with the wee body and the huge cock, wasn't just two-timing his wife, but your sister as well, in your flat. Because he sure was diddling her. She wrote and told you all about him. Nijinsky, remember?' That was what I thought. But what I said was, 'Okay love, let's check that out. She was with a theatre company, yes?'

She looked at me gratefully. 'Yes, the Lyceum, usually.'

'Right, we'll go there this morning. I've got a couple of quick interviews. I can do them both by ten-thirty, and type them up later, after we've been to the theatre and after we give our statements to Dylan.

'Meantime, let's see what the papers say.' We had picked up a *Scotsman* and a *Daily Record* at Ali's. With little to go on, each paper gave the story inside-page treatment, reporting that the police were still trying to identify a man found stabbed to death in a flat in Ebeneezer Street. He was described as around forty, portly, and around five feet four inches in height.

It struck me, idly, that if we handed the fiver to Archer, and sold our story to the *Record*, we would make more than the ten per cent cut on offer. It came to me also, forcefully, through the enshrouding mist of love, that as well we would stand to do at least six months each for wasting police time, withholding information, stealing evidence, and anything else the Clever Bastards chose to chuck at us.

I gulped, and looked down at Prim, her head resting happily against my chest, her hand lying innocently on the outside of my thigh. I decided that I would keep the dangers of our tightrope walk across the chasm of uncertainty strictly to myself.

'The things you do for love, Oz,' I whispered. She heard me and smiled up, quizzically. As she did, her hand moved fractionally on my thigh. I stood up quickly, before she found out, before she was ready, that it's true what they say about us Scots guys, even when our kilts are made of towelling.

In which we meet a camp follower
and learn of Dawn's big break.

I'm not exactly a regular theatregoer. Every so often I've been persuaded by a lady to take her to one of the big musicals they put on for long runs at the Playhouse, but live events are not really my thing. That said, on the few occasions when I have been lured along there, the Lyceum has always struck me as a nice wee hall. It's got a friendly feel about it; it isn't grandiose like the Festival Theatre, or such a big barn of a place that the sound bends into funny shapes if you're sat up in the Gods.

When we parked in Grindlay Street, I jumped out of the car and headed off towards the glazed foyer. I thought that Prim had fallen in behind me, but she stopped me with a whistle. '*Wow, she can even whistle,*' I thought.

'Not there,' she said, 'the offices are across the street.' So instead, I followed her, watching her skirt swish from side to side with the delicious movement of her explosive hips.

The administration and rehearsal rooms of the Lyceum were up a close, and behind an anonymous door. There was no obvious reception area and so we wandered along a corridor, looking for signs of life. The corridor ended in a double door. I looked at Prim, shrugged my shoulders and opened it, gently and slowly.

We stepped into a big room with a few chairs and other odds and ends of furniture scattered haphazardly around. In its centre, a man sat, with his back to us. He hadn't heard us come in and stayed in his seat, bent over as if reading something in his lap.

I felt that a theatrical cough was appropriate. The bloke straightened up with a start, then twisted in his chair to peer over his shoulder at us. He wore glasses and had a long nose. The way he stared, I formed the distinct impression that he was looking down it at us. And I didn't like that much. 'Yeasss?' he said, in a voice that rang with luvvieness. 'Are we lost, little people?'

I don't like being patronised at the best of times, and especially not by a tall, disjointed pillock with limp wrists, long, highlighted hair, a shirt with a frayed collar and a sweater that looked like an insect colony. 'No, chum,' I said, trying my best to sound like a private eye, 'we're not. But we're looking for someone who could be.'

He stood up. His jeans were even scruffier than his shirt and sweater. 'Indeed. And who might that be?'

Prim stepped forward, smiling her sweetest. 'My sister actually, Dawn Phillips. I'm Primavera. I've just got back from Africa and I've no idea where she is.' She waved a hand vaguely at me. 'This is Oz Blackstone, my boyfriend.' My heart swelled with pride, knowing that today it was pretty close to the truth.

'Ah,' said the thespian, 'once more, the fragile Dawn. I don't know if I'll be of much help to you, but I'll do my best.'

His tone was different. It's funny, but Prim is one of those people that it's just impossible to patronise, as Dylan had discovered, the hard way.

'I am Rawdon Brooks,' he said, with the briefest of courtly bows. '*What a prat!*' I thought. 'I am the Artistic Director of this humble repertory. Normally, Primavera – what a wonderful name – you would find Dawn here or close by, but not today, I'm afraid.

'We have a visiting company in the Lyceum at the moment. We don't go into rehearsal for another ten days. During that time, your sister should be making her big breakthrough into moviedom. Far from being lost, you could say she's been discovered.

'There are some Americans around, making one of these awful kilt and claymore things. *Son of Rob Roy* or some such nonsense. Dawn has a small part in it, but she'll get billing for it. She's playing a camp follower . . .' '*A bit like you then,*' I almost said. '. . . or something, dressed up in a scanty plaid, I should imagine, and being ravished by the fearful Redcoats.'

'Billy Butlin's got a lot to answer for,' I muttered, but Brooks was in full declaiming mode.

'The trouble with these operations is that they shoot to a tight schedule, moving around all over the place. One day here, next day there, the day after, God knows where. So, while I am sure that she will be somewhere north of Perth – if she has scenes today, that is – I have no idea exactly where that would be.'

As you may have gathered, I'm the sort of guy who's big on first impressions, and this man had triggered off a creeping dislike in me. I did my best to suppress it. 'When did this gig begin? How long has she been away?'

'Since the beginning of last week.'

'So she's been out of town for the last ten days or so?' said Prim, questioning.

'That's possible, my dear, but she could have been back, then off again. As I said she has but a small part. It's unlikely she'd be shooting every day, and in Scotland – fearful place that it is – the wilderness is only a couple of hours away.'

I'm no rabid nationalist, but that was too much for me. 'Come on, pal. Wilderness! Ever heard of Moss Side?'

He looked at me, down that long nose again. 'Mmm. A touchy Jock, is he? Your wilderness is earning your country millions of dollars, my dear boy. You shouldn't be ashamed of it.'

'I'm not. But this "fearful" place is feeding you right now, so maybe you should show it more respect. And I warn you, if you say anything smart about pearls and swine, I shall kick you sharply in the balls . . . my dear.'

Brooks laughed and threw up his long flapping hands. 'Pax! Pax! I must stop provoking you chaps, or I really will get into trouble. The fellow yesterday was just as upset as you, but he was a policeman, so I got away with it.'

'I wouldn't bet on it. You'd better be careful where you park your car. What policeman was this, then?'

'He called here yesterday. He said he was CID, and he was asking questions about Dawn, too. I hope the child is all right. She's your sister,' he said to Prim, 'so you'll know how sensitive she can be. Just lately she's been very emotional. Every so often a spontaneous weep, other times unnaturally cheerful. I asked her if she had something on her mind, but she wouldn't say.'

'This copper,' I asked. 'Was he alone?'

'Yes, quite.'

'What time did he call?'

Brooks scratched the stubble on his chin. 'Just after I got in. Must have been around ten-fifteen.'

'What was his name?'

'You know, he didn't say.'

'Did he show you ID?'

'I didn't think to ask. It upsets them, you know. One doesn't like to provoke.'

'Can you describe him then?'

The actor laughed again. 'My dear boy, I have always assumed that policemen are called pigs because they all look exactly alike. He was just another aggressive chap in a raincoat, that's all.

'But tell me, why do you ask?'

Before I could conjure up a half-decent lie, Prim jumped in. 'Dawn was involved with a policeman for a while. He didn't like it when she chucked him, and he gave her a hard time.'

'Then she should complain to his superiors, surely.'

'That could be asking for even more trouble,' she said. 'You can't think of any quick way for us to trace Dawn, then, other than driving around the Highlands looking for movie lights?'

Brooks paused for a second or two. 'There's a company called Celtic Scenery, based down in Leith somewhere. They maintain a database of potential film sites. Visiting companies use them for advance work, choosing locations to suit story-lines, making sure that there are no electricity pylons in the background of the highland heroes, that sort of thing.' I smiled briefly to myself, remembering jet trails in the sky in a B-movie Western that I'd seen on TV as a kid. 'If they've been involved, they might have a copy of the shooting schedule.

'That's as much help as I can give you. Now I must return to my script.' He turned his back on us abruptly and rearranged himself, artistically, on his chair.

'Thank you very much, Mr Brooks,' said Prim. Without turning, he waved a hand, feebly. We made our way back into the corridor and out of the building.

The morning sunshine was refreshing after the gloom of the rehearsal room. 'What an arsehole that guy is!' I spluttered as we emerged.

'Ah, my darling,' said Prim. 'That's your inherent Scottish homophobia coming out.'

I looked at her in surprise. 'Homoph . . . So you reckon he is too?'

'As queer as a nineteen pound note, so Dawn said in one of her letters. It used to be a three pound note: that's inflation for you, eh?'

I thought about it. 'No, I won't have the term homophobia used about me. I've never been afraid of a homosexual in my life. I'm a liberal in that respect. A couple of my best friends are gay. That bloke in there could be as straight as an arrow and he'd still be an arsehole.'

'I agree,' she said, 'but he was useful though. Celtic Scenery can be our next stop, after we see Dylan. Could he have been the policeman who visited Brooks, d'you think?'

'Not unless he was hell of a quick on his feet. Mike Dylan was at Leith to respond to Constable McArse's call only a few minutes after Brooks had his visit. And why would he have been asking questions about Dawn *before* Kane's body was found?

'There's no saying it was a policeman anyway. He was on his own, which isn't right. Brooks didn't see a warrant card, or even ask to see one.'

Prim smiled, mischievously. 'He was probably too busy having fantasies about truncheons.'

'Unworthy! No, that could have been anyone. It could even

have been the real killer.' A shudder swept through me. 'In fact, it probably was!'

Her eyes lit up. 'And if that's the case, it means that Dawn must have got away from him.'

'Aye, but it also means that he's looking for her. We'd better get a move on. Let's go back to the loft and see if we can find an address for Celtic Scenery in Good Old *Yellow Pages*.'

In which Prim says 'Hello Mum',
and the quest goes on.

GOYP let us down for once, but the good old Royal Mail Postal Address book turned up trumps. Celtic Scenery was listed at a quayside address in Leith Docks, less than a mile from the police station in Queen Charlotte Street, where we were to meet Dylan.

We sat on the sofa, clothed this time. At our feet, Wallace's endless pursuit of the sun had taken him to a square in the middle of the varnished wooden floor where he sprawled contentedly, crunching away at a bowl of Wonder Weinie Iguana Superfood.

I put the Royal Mail book back in a drawer in my desk. 'Ready to go?' I asked Primavera.

She stood up. 'Yes, but can I make a quick call first, to my Mum. I should have called yesterday, but with one thing and another . . .'

'Sure, you do that, I'll leave you to it.'

'No, you wait right here.'

She picked up the black handset and punched a telephone

number into the dialling panel, fidgeting nervously as it rang out.

'Mum?' Her face lit up with a huge smile. 'It's me. I'm back home. Yes, I'm safe, and I'm well. In fact, I'm better than I've been in years.' She paused. 'Why should you leap to that conclusion? Yes, I am; but we're friends that's all. Yes, he's here. I'm at his place in fact . . . Don't "Oh yes" me, Mother!'

She glanced up at me. 'His name's Oz Blackstone and he's daft. Here Oz, say hello to Mum.' She thrust the phone at me.

'Hello Mrs Phillips,' I said to British Telecom, 'how are you?'

'Very well, thank you Oz.' Her voice sounded hearty, in a country sort of way. 'So you're daft, are you. In that case you and Primavera should get on very well together. She sounds very happy.'

I tried to think of an appropriate answer. 'I think she is, Mrs Phillips. There's no accounting for taste. Here she is again.' I returned the phone to Prim.

'Mum, we've got to go out right now, but we'll come up to see you as soon as we can. Let's see how the weekend goes. Yes, he is. 'Bye.'

She hung up. 'Mum said you sound charming.' She kissed me, quickly. I kissed her in return, more slowly.

For a second or two her body moulded itself against mine, until she pulled herself away and held me at arm's length. 'Oz, I told you, first things first. My sister's in trouble, and it's up to you and I to find her.'

In which we tell porkies for the record, pick up Dawn's trail, and discover that the law isn't as big an ass as it looks.

Prim's phone call had made it impossible for us to fit in Celtic Scenery before the police, and so we headed directly for the Leith Station, a drab Victorian building in Queen Charlotte Street.

I went up to the bar of the general office and introduced myself, and Prim, to the constable on duty. 'DI Dylan's expecting us,' I told her. She looked at me in what I took for slight surprise. 'Take a seat over there,' she ordered, pointing. I looked at the uncomfortable wooden bench and decided to disobey.

A few minutes later a businesslike young man in his mid-twenties appeared through a half-glazed door labelled 'Private'.

'Good morning,' he said, although incorrect by a few minutes. 'I'm Detective Constable Morrow. Mr Dylan's apologies, but he had to go out on enquiries. He's asked me to take your statements. He said it was just a formality.'

He led us through to a small, windowless, airless interview room. It smelled of earlier occupants, and I guessed it was that special kind of room you hear about in police stations, with walls which move about on occasions; such as when a suspect proves difficult, or provocative.

Morrow was a nice lad, and actually meant it when he apologised for the conditions. 'We have all this high-tech stuff now,' he said, 'yet we still have to interview ordinary decent folk like you in smelly wee rooms like this.'

He asked us only the most basic questions, allowing us to tell our stories unprompted to the tape recorder. We were lying for the record this time, and that worried me, more than slightly. But with Archer's secret, my doubts about him, and Dawn's predicament whirling about in my mind, I plunged on, comforting myself with the hope that one part of our story might well become true, even if retrospectively.

It didn't take long. When I was a trainee copper, I'd had to take my statements down in longhand in a daft wee notebook, in the knowledge that I might have to read them aloud in court. I had heard tales of what could happen to policemen in the witness box, and afterwards in the Chief Constable's office if their jotters had been doctored in any way. 'Let me see your notebook, officer,' is the last thing any Plod wants to hear the judge say when he's up there, in the box, under oath. My book was always impeccable, but for all that I was still a pretty awful copper.

'Thank you very much,' said young Morrow, when we had finished talking to the tape. 'I'll have these transcribed, then I'll ask you to sign them. It'll take about twenty minutes, half an hour at most. You can either wait, or look in again later. It's up to you.'

'We'll come back in,' I said, taking an executive decision. 'Will you be ready by one?'

He nodded, and showed us out through the front office and

into the street, where yet another traffic warden was prowling around my car. We jumped in quick and drove off, leaving her scowling in frustration.

It took us a while to find Celtic Scenery. You don't expect to find business offices right on a dockside, but that's where it was, tucked in behind the Malmaison Hotel, not far from the radio station.

The entire resources of the company turned out to be two networked computers, and two bright, energetic young women. This time, I left the talking to Prim.

The ladies looked at us in surprise as we entered. I guessed that theirs was a business which attracted few customers to the door. There was no counter and only one spare chair. We stood there awkwardly for a few seconds, until they stood up and came round from behind their desks.

'Hi,' said Prim. 'I hope you can help us.' She fished in her handbag and produced a driving licence. 'I'm looking for my sister, on a very urgent family matter. She's an actress; her name's Dawn Phillips. And here's mine, look.' She held out the driving licence for the women to inspect. They looked at it, but the suspicion on their faces was unwavering.

Prim ploughed on, using everything she had to establish her credibility. 'Rawdon Brooks, at the Lyceum, sent us down to see you. He told us that Dawn has a part in an American movie that's being shot on location over here. He couldn't remember the name, but he said it was a Highland epic, and he thought that you might have been involved with them.'

The women looked at each other, then at Prim, then at me, then at each other again. Finally one of them nodded, and went back to her work-station, leaving the other to deal with us. She was stocky and confident, dressed in jeans, a tee-shirt and sandals.

'It sounds like the remake of *Kidnapped*,' she said. 'It's Miles Grayson's new project. He's playing the lead and directing as usual. It's the second time he's used us to do set-ups for him.' Her face shone with professional pride. I wasn't surprised. Apart, maybe, from the President of the United States, the Pope and the Queen, Miles Grayson is the most famous human on the planet.

'We don't see the cast list,' the woman went on, 'so I can't tell you if your sister's there or not, but yes, we do know where they'll be today.' She paused. 'Look, it would be more than my life was worth to send you to the set, but I'll take a chance and tell you that they're booked into the Falls of Lora Hotel, in Connell Ferry, tonight and tomorrow.'

'Could we phone the hotel and check whether Dawn's there?' asked Prim.

The woman shook her head. 'No. We made a block booking for them, and they won't have checked in yet. If it's as urgent as all that you'll just have to go up there to look for her. It's not that long a drive, actually. Go via Bridge of Earn and you'll do it in about three hours.'

We thanked the girls and went back out to the dock. There was a breeze coming in off the sea. We stood there and looked around, across the grey-blue river mouth to the Waterfront Bistro, and beyond, to the new Government office building, in all its white awfulness. We grabbed a coke and a quick sandwich in the Malmaison Bar, then drove back up to the police station, parking this time outside the bakery in Elbe Street, seeking sanctuary from the wardens.

Young Morrow was in the front office as we entered the old building, at about twenty past one. 'Sorry,' I said, 'did we keep you from your lunch?' He smiled and shook his head, giving me the impression that lunch was for wimps.

'Here you are; they're all typed up and ready. There's no need to go through to the Black Hole again. If you'll just read them and sign them, that'll be it.'

We did as we were told. I gulped inwardly as I put my pen to our economies with the truth. 'How's the investigation going?' I asked, by way of conversation.

Morrow looked at me, unsmiling for the first time. He leaned towards me and whispered, so that only I could hear. 'The boss said to me that you used to be one of us, so I'll tell you. We identified the guy an hour ago. His name's William Kane. He's a stockbroker. He left his wife a wee while back, for another woman. The wife says she doesn't know who it was, but Dylan's going on the assumption that it was your girlfriend's sister. So if she shows up, we're going to want to speak to her.'

I winced with a show of concern. 'Shit!' I said quietly. 'Thanks for that. I can't believe that Dawn would get herself involved in that kind of situation, but don't worry, if she shows up in town I'll bring her to see you myself.'

We turned to leave. My hand was on the doorknob when he called after us. 'Oh! Miss Phillips, I almost forgot. Mr Dylan told me to ask you about that torn fiver you picked up yesterday. He said that technically he shouldn't have let you take anything from the house, so he asks, could he have it back for now?'

Prim looked at the young detective, all sweetness and blushing innocence. 'I'm really sorry,' she said, 'but I taped the two halves together and spent it. On groceries, I think. Inspector Dylan won't get into trouble, will he?' Morrow smiled grimly, as if trouble for Mike Dylan wouldn't bother him too much.

'Let's hope not,' he said, untruthfully.

In which we have a visitor,
and Ali does too.

Heavy clouds covered the sun when we stepped out into Queen Charlotte Street. It looked as though the weather was about to break. As I drove back up Leith Walk towards the Old Town, we talked tactics, and agreed that we would head straight for the Falls of Lora Hotel. By the reckoning of the girl in Celtic Scenery, and it was her business to know these things, we would be there by five-thirty.

I looked up at the belvedere as I drew up to my parking space. 'That's funny. Old Wallace must think the sun's still shining.' Prim followed my gaze. Our loftmate was sprawled out along the window ledge, pressed to the glass as if he was trying to reach some sunshine just outside.

'You going to like living with an iguana?' I asked my new flatmate, as I parked.

'Oz my dear, if I can cope with you, I could cope with a tyrannosaurus.' She smiled. There's something about Prim's smile that goes straight to my knees. You can see right through it into her heart, and know that she's happy. It's the sort of smile that made it seem right then as if the sun was still shining inside my old Nissan, for me alone. She kissed me quickly on the cheek and jumped out of the car.

We knew that something was wrong as soon as we stepped through the front door, and saw the kitchen. All of the contents of the cupboards were laid out along the breakfast bar, every last tin of beans, every last jar of herbs.

'Bloody hell,' I said. 'Those mice are getting too bloody cheeky for their own good!'

Prim beat me up the stairs, but only just. Her cry of alarm was still hanging in the air as I reached the living area. 'Ransacked' is a word I'd never used in my life until then. There's nothing else in the *OED* quite like it, and when you think of it, it's as descriptive as you can get. Everything I, everything we, had was laid out in neat piles. Prim's bag was empty, on the floor. Her clothes had all been turned inside out. A dozen tampons in their paper casing were lined up neatly beside their box. I think that, more than anything else, was what made her cry.

All of the cupboard doors lay open. The drawers of my desk were stacked upon its surface, one on another. Even the lining of Wallace's cage had been disturbed.

Ever seen an outraged iguana? That's the only way I can describe the look on his face as my dinosaur appeared down the ladder from the belvedere. He glared around the room in human indignation, then at us, as if to say, 'What the hell's this then?'

Prim saw him and all at once her tears, which had been making my shirt decidedly damp, turned into laughter.

'Poor old chap,' she said, jumping on to the sleeping level, and for the first time in either of their lives, picking him up. The old bugger swelled with pride. I'll swear that he nuzzled his head against her breast. Imagine, for a fleeting second I was jealous of an iguana. She carried him down, and separated some food from the pile on the floor, putting the rest back into its box. As she did, she looked up at me.

'Who did it, Oz, do you think? Were they looking for . . .' My nod cut off her sentence unfinished.

'What else? Or did you smuggle some uncut diamonds back from Africa? As far as "who's" concerned, who knows about the fiver? Mike Dylan asked about it, but that doesn't prove that he understands what it's about. It's quite possible young Morrow's story was straight up, and that Dylan was just trying to cover up a mistake.

'No, the only people we know of who understand what that fiver's really worth are Ray Archer and your sister, although it's possible that Dawn only opened the account, and doesn't know what's in it.'

Prim shook her head and stood up, leaving Wallace munching on the floor. 'There could be another.'

'Who's that?'

'The mystery man who was looking for Dawn before we found Kane's body.'

'True, unless that was Ray Archer – and it could have been. Whoever it was, he still doesn't have the fiver, does he. And with the sort of dough it unlocks at stake, somehow I don't think he's going to give up looking.

'The safest thing we can do, love, is go to see Mike Dylan, give him the fiver and tell him the whole story. If we were lucky he'd only charge us with wasting police time.'

She squeezed my arm. 'I know that, but . . .'

I cut her off again. It's a bad habit of mine. 'Yes, I know. That would land Dawn right in it. Even if she could prove she was out of town when Kane was killed, she could still be charged as a party to theft, for opening that bank account. The police, and nine juries out of ten, would assume that she knew what Kane was going to do.

'There's also the small matter,' I added, 'of our cut from Ray Archer for picking up the money.'

'Except that if you're right and if Archer is involved in Kane's death, that cut might be our throats.' Primavera has a wonderful knack of getting to the nub of a situation. 'So what are we going to do, Oz?'

'The same thing we set out to do this morning. Find your sister, before someone else does. Leave this place exactly as it is just now. Let's stuff that bag of yours with enough clothes for a few days, arrange an iguana sitter, and head on up to Connell Ferry.'

She nodded and began to pack. Five minutes later, we closed the door behind us. This time, I locked the mortice as well as the Yale. We looked around as we stepped into the street, as ready as we could be for anything, but no-one was watching us that we could see. I threw our bag in the boot of the car and turned the key in the lock, then taking Prim by the hand, I led the way up to the High Street.

As I looked down the street before crossing, I thought I saw a familiar Armani suit in the distance.

'Hullaw ther youse two. Enjoy the breakfast then? Mair sausage for lunch, or is it back tae the tuna rolls?' I shook my head and explained to Ali that we had decided to go away for a couple of days. Some people think that I take a hell of a chance asking Ali to look after Wallace, but that's a racist slur. I happen to know that he's very particular about what he puts into his curries.

I handed him my spare key, then took a flyer. 'You just had the police in here?'

'Aye. Did you see the bastard? It was that flash boy Dylan, him that's in the papers a' the time. He came marchin' in saying something about fake banknotes, and wantin' tae check the cash in the till. Cheeky sod. Accusin' me of handling bent money! He had a look through it, but he didnae find anything. 'S as well he didnae come yesterday. Ma lunchtime relief took a tenner that was practically still wet. Ah wis dead lucky. Got rid of it in change tae a whisky salesman!'

Smiling at Ali's good fortune, and mulling over all the possible connections between Dylan's official search, Prim's off-the-cuff fabrication to young Morrow, and our visitor with the ability to open Yale locks without a key we jumped into the Nissan as fast as we could and put the old grey streets of Edinburgh behind us.

'Why would Dylan lie to Ali?' Prim murmured, eventually, as we passed the towering bowl of Murrayfield on our way out of the City. 'Why would he spin him a line about fake money, when all the time he knows that he's looking for just one particular note? All he had to say was that the note was evidence in a case.'

Smart girl, my Primavera, isn't she. I glanced at my watch, which told me that I had known her now for over twenty-eight hours. A day and a bit. The longest day and a bit of my life, the most memorable, and even if we didn't come through this whole business intact, the greatest. We were flying, Primavera Phillips and I, high on adrenalin, high on the thrill of the chase. And we were flying too, from a city where danger lived. More than likely we were quarry ourselves, in the eye of someone with the ruthlessness and the physical strength to ram that knife all the way up into wee Willie (or big Willie, if you want to look at it that way) Kane's head. Now, I guessed, we had what that someone wanted, the key to a bank vault containing a serious amount of hot, and once it was moved on, untraceable money.

'Why's Dylan after the fiver in the first place?' I said. 'The boy Morrow was right. Technically he shouldn't have let us take anything out of that house, in case it had an essential print on it or a piece of DNA. Maybe he's embarrassed by that. But if he is, why stir the thing up? The best way for him to cover his tracks is just to forget about it.

'Instead, he has Morrow ask us about the fiver. Yet he's so keen to get it back that at the same time he takes the chance of breaking into the loft and turning it inside out.'

She looked at me in astonishment. 'You think Dylan did that?'

'Aye, of course he did. Policemen know a thousand ways of opening lockfast places as quick as you like without making a mess. And whoever did the loft went through two locked doors, the one to the street and m . . .' I caught myself. '. . . ours,' She smiled and squeezed my hand at the plural, 'without leaving a mark. Point one, a real housebreaker would have gone straight through the door with a crowbar, point two, would not have been daft enough to try the street door in the daylight, and point three, would have had no way of knowing that the loft was empty. Last and finally, point four, straight after the break-in Dylan walks into Ali's, just round the corner, and talks his way through the till. What's the betting he'd just phoned young Morrow?'

'Aghast' is another of my favourite words, but I'd never seen anyone looking that way until Prim looked at me in the car. 'But that's desperate!' she gasped. 'Why would he do all that?'

'Either because someone's cut him in on the deal, or because someone's put the fear of God into him over his career prospects if he doesn't get the fiver back, having broken procedure by letting you take it from the flat.'

'But who could do that?'

I opened my mouth, the usual smart-arsed 'Ah, my dear, that is the sixty-four dollar question!' hanging on the edge of my tongue. And all at once I knew. I saw for certain who could put the fear of God in Mike Dylan. I saw too, that he was not a man to concern himself unduly with a trivial oversight. He didn't want that fiver back as a point of principle. He wanted it for what it was. Oh no: whatever the incentive, it came to me that the threat that had shaken the creases out of Dylan's Armani suit had issued straight from the mouth of the man who had killed Willie Kane. '*Smart bastard, that Blackstone!*' you may be thinking, but I knew him all right, in that very moment, and for the first time since I had walked into Prim's flat and discovered the befouled corpse on her bed, I was scared. Really scared for me, but absolutely terrified for Prim. Dylan I could cope with. Dylan was a clown, a slightly bent and mentally limited copper, but no threat. But this guy . . .

Prim was looking at me. Her aghastness had changed to expectation. My hands gripping the wheel as I turned towards the M8 junction, I smiled, sideways, the first and last insincere smile I've ever given her.

'Ah, my dear,' I said, 'that is the sixty-four dollar question!'

She laughed and punched my arm. 'Oz, that's my first disappointment. I thought you had an answer for everything!'

In which the fourth most famous
human on the planet
buys us a drink.

We made a deal that on the journey to Connell Ferry we would forget Dylan, torn fivers and the rest. The amazing thing was that just by being with each other we could do that. We chatted about nothings, funny experiences from our lives. We sketched in the broad facts of our previous love-lives, without either of us feeling any strange pangs.

I filled Prim in on the basics of my relationship with Jan. She tutted in disapproval when I admitted that my last live-in had left after she found out that under the influence of a few bevvies, I had admitted to Ali that my nickname for her was 'Tomorrow'. It was a cruel thing and I'm not proud of it. I didn't have to spell out the punchline for Prim.

A daft thought came to me as I drove along, casting off the shackles of prehistory. 'All my past life now,' I said grandly, 'I'll call BP, Before Primavera.'

She laughed spontaneously, brightly, joyously, doubling over in the driver's seat and holding her sides. 'You can't do that,' she spluttered, 'or all of mine will have been BO!'

It wasn't that funny, but tension made us laugh so hard, that I had to pull the car into a parking place. We sat there, our chests heaving from our mirth . . . heaving very provocatively in Prim's case, I have to say. Occasionally one of us would look at the other, and we would break out again. Eventually, I reached across and held her shoulders, and as I did a feeling came over me, as yet another emotional height was scaled. 'In that case, my love, since acronyms are out, all my life till now has been Winter. I've spent it waiting for my Springtime, and now she's here.' I was only slightly surprised when I realised that Mr Lump was back in my throat.

She looked at me and smiled. 'You're really laying it on the line, aren't you,' she whispered. 'Just give me time. That's all I ask.'

After a while we drove on, heading towards the West, watching as the leafy countryside gave way to moorland, and as the surrounding hills grew into mountains. Eventually a salty tang came into the air and flooded the car through Prim's open window.

'God, but you don't know how good the taste of this is, my dear, daft Oz, after twelve months of Africa. The heat, the poverty, the cruelty, the blood. I never ever want to go back to that place again.'

'What, not even to minister to the sick?' The old Oz was disappearing. There wasn't a trace of irony in my question.

I glanced across at her. She was sitting with her legs pulled up on the squab, grasping her neat ankles. She shook her head slowly and deliberately. 'No way on Earth. I've hit the compassion wall too, just like my late pal. I left the hospice for a different world, and what I found was far, far worse. I can't take it any more. Sister Phillips has hung up her starched bunnet for good and all.

'Although I haven't a clue what I'm going to do next!'

'Don't do anything, then. I can look after us both.'

She flashed me a glance, suddenly sharp and serious. 'Don't even think that, far less say it. I'll consider living with the right man, although that's something I've never done before. But I'll always want my identity, and working is part of it. What if you and I got together, and it wore off, or something? Where would I be?'

'Primavera,' I said, 'when it wears off for me it'll be because your zimmer keeps on blocking the stair up to the loft; and even then I'll just rig up a pulley and haul you straight up to the balcony.'

She took a hand from her ankles and rubbed it, gentle as silk over the back of my hand on the steering wheel. We drove on for a while, safe in our island away from the action, and the danger.

'Where are we going to stay tonight?' asked Prim.

'That kind of depends on whether or not we find your sister, doesn't it. Let's play it by ear.'

Connell Ferry's a bit of a misnomer, because there's a bridge there, a big iron single-track thing that was built in the days when, even north of Oban, the prospect of today's traffic volumes would have looked like visions from one of H. G. Wells' wilder efforts. We saw it well before we reached the village, and slowed up, looking for the Falls of Lora Hotel.

It wasn't hard to find. It's a big building on the left, as you come into the village; once it was someone's grand house, no doubt, but extended now, in a totally uncomplementary style. The car park looked as if it might have been a cowshed once, but now it was empty, save for a Land Rover with the Falls of Lora logo on its spare-wheel cover.

I parked the Nissan under the curving roof, and jumped out.

103

Prim took my arm, as we crunched along the gravel towards the entrance.

The reception area was small, and empty. There was nothing fancy about it, just a dark-varnished counter in the shadow of the staircase, with a doorway leading off. Prim pushed the service bell, and after a few minutes a girl appeared, fresh-faced and not far out of her teens, wearing what looked like a waitress's uniform.

'Yes?' she said, in a lovely island lilt. 'Can I help you?'

All at once my mind swam back to a night in the cocktail bar of another hotel, in St Andrews, with my Dad and his sailor pal Archie. The girl there was as fresh-faced as this one, with an accent as soft as mist, and as wild as heather. Archie said to her, 'Where are you from, then?'

'Tiree,' the lass replied.

'Ah,' said the old salt. 'They'll have had to lasso you to get you over here, then!'

Back in the present, Prim said, 'I hope so. I'm looking for my sister. She's with the film party, and I understand they're booked in here. Have they arrived yet?'

'Not yet,' said the girl. 'We're expecting them any time now, though. Why don't you wait in the bar. It's just through there.' She pointed along a narrow hallway to her left.

'Okay.' Prim took my hand and started off along the corridor, but I held her back, gently. 'Suppose we wanted to stay tonight,' I asked, 'have you any room left?'

The girl shook her head. 'Sorry. The film party have booked the whole place.

'But there are plenty of hotels down in Oban,' she added, doing her best to please. 'You'll get booked in there all right.'

We made our way through to the bar. It was a big room, square but for an alley off one corner, where a dartboard hung on the wall. A big open fireplace was set in its centre, topped by a copper flue which disappeared up into the roof. Prim took a seat in the corner, near the window. 'What would you like to drink, love?' I asked her.

'Just a lime and soda. If they have any sandwiches, I wouldn't mind one. It seems forever since lunch.'

I pressed the service bell; after only a second or two, a door opened behind the bar, and the young receptionist appeared. 'Jesus,' I said, 'they work you hard.'

She shrugged her shoulders. 'Och, I like it. You get to meet all sorts of interesting people.'

'Aye, I can imagine,' I said. 'A right wee metropolis Connell Ferry must be.'

Prim and I sat together in the bar, munching thick crab sandwiches and looking northward out of the window, across the narrow mouth of Loch Etive, with the great Bens rising in the distance. 'It's amazing how insular people can be.' She was speaking a thought aloud. 'I've been to five European countries. I've straddled the equator. Yet here I am in Scotland in a place I've never seen before, in a different country to the one I thought I knew.'

'You and me both,' I said, slipping an arm around her waist. 'You and me and thousands of our country-folk. Most central-belt Jocks get panic attacks as soon as they leave a built-up area. All this "Flower of Scotland" stuff is so much crap, you know. Our nation is like everywhere else in the world, a collection of tribes and villages, each one holding on to its own and living in suspicion and fear of its neighbours.'

'That's very profound, Osbert.'

I sipped my Coke and smiled, a touch self-consciously. 'The mask slips occasionally. Just don't tell anyone.'

She smiled and kissed my cheek. 'I promise. The serious

Oz is someone I'll keep to myself.'

As she spoke, the door from the corridor creaked open, and in the same moment, the receptionist-barmaid-waitress appeared behind the beer-taps without being summoned by bell.

We recognised him at once, as soon as he stepped into the room. Miles Grayson was an impressive guy on screen. But I knew he had to be forty-something, and I had a cynical view of what he would look like close-up, once the make-up was stripped away. Come to think of it, I have the same cynical view of all actors and politicians. I was wrong about this bloke.

My Dad has a great saying, applied most often to our current Head of Government, 'He seems to make a room bigger just by being in it.' Miles Grayson was the opposite. He was one of those rare human beings who shrink the space around them. Even as he was then, tired after a long day, the vitality came from him in waves. He wasn't very tall, around five ten, I guessed, but he carried himself like someone six inches taller. He was wearing black denim and black hiking boots, every inch the New Age Cowboy. He looked across and smiled at us, and automatically Prim and I nodded back, mouths hanging slightly open.

He turned to the barmaid and melted her with The Smile. 'Is that Fosters cold, honey?' She nodded vigorously, speechless. 'I mean like really cold?' I thought the lassie's neck would snap. 'Okay, then I'll have a pint, in a straight glass please.'

Prim tugged my arm and whispered in my ear. 'What do we do now?'

'Seems like a good idea to let the man get outside his pint, then we'll see.'

Grayson solved our problem. 'What can I get you?' he called across the bar.

'I'll have one of them, thanks.' I pointed at the Fosters. 'How about you, love?'

'Lime and soda, thanks,' said Prim.

The movie star turned barman, bringing the drinks across on a metal tray. 'Do you two live here?' he asked, as he sat down beside us. His accent was strange, a blend of Aussie, American and received pronunciation from drama school.

'No,' I said. 'Edinburgh. How about you?' Cheeky bastard, Blackstone, but I couldn't resist it. Grayson's right eyebrow twitched, and he smiled, not taken aback in the slightest. 'Sorry,' I said. 'Cheers.' I took a swallow of the Fosters. The girl was right. It was icy.

I put the glass down and held out my hand. 'My name's Oz Blackstone, and this is Prim Phillips.

'You finished work for the day?'

Grayson ignored my question. Like many celebrities, he had perfected the royal art of acknowledging hundreds, even thousands of people simultaneously, putting out his own presence but absorbing none of theirs. Now it was as if he was looking at Prim for the first time. 'Phillips,' he repeated.

'Yes,' said Prim. 'You might know my sister, Dawn. I think she's working on your film.'

He looked at her, and a smile lit up his face. 'Yeah, I know Dawn. In fact only three days ago I made wild, abandoned love to her . . . but only for the cameras, worse luck. She's a tough nut to crack, is Dawn.

'So you're her sister. The one with the great name. She told me about you, but she said you were in Africa.'

'So I was, until Wednesday. I thought it'd be a nice idea for us to surprise Dawn. Is she here?'

Grayson looked at her, curiously, for a while, as if he was considering his answer. At last he shook his head. 'No, she isn't. She has a few days between scenes, and she asked me on Wednesday if she could take some time away. She left that same morning.' His eyebrows rose, as if in anticipation. 'She is due back on Monday, though.'

'Dammit,' said Prim, frowning. 'She didn't say where she was going, did she?'

'No. She only said that she had some things to sort out, and needed a few days. I was disappointed, because I thought we'd been getting on pretty well together, but I said okay, because I could tell that she meant it.

'I rate your sister in every respect, Miss Phillips. Quite apart from turning me on every time she walks on set, she's a damn fine actress. In fact, I've told her writers to expand her part. This movie will make her a star. Then maybe she'll have time for me. Like I said, she's a hard nut to crack.'

He caught something in Prim's eye. 'Hey, I'm legit, honest. I came out of a relationship about a year back.'

A thought struck me. 'I thought you were doing a remake of *Kidnapped.*'

'Yeah, that's right,' said Grayson. 'Great story, ain't it.'

'So who are you playing? With respect, you're a bit mature for young David Balfour.'

'Just a bit, yeah. No, I'm playing Allan Breck. He's the real hero, after all. Why d'you ask?'

'No reason, really. It's just that when I read *Kidnapped* at school, I don't remember Allan Breck getting his leg over. I don't remember there being any sort of a part for an actress, either, far less one that could be expanded.'

Miles Grayson spread his arms wide, with a grin that was as honest and disarming as the midsummer day was long. 'Come on, guy, this is Hollywood. We're out to entertain. The reason *Kidnapped* hasn't been a hit before is that it's been made like the story, a Buddy movie. You want to put bums on seats, like you say over here, you need some love interest.'

I shook my head. 'Aye, man, fair enough. But next time you're in Samoa, make sure you visit Robert Louis Stevenson's grave. If you put your ear to the ground I'm sure you'll hear him spinning round in his coffin.

'What's next? Long John Silver with two legs, so you can work in a tap-dance routine.'

The actor laughed. 'Hey, Oz! How did you know I used to be a dancer?'

We were still laughing when the door behind us creaked once more. A harassed, bald, fat man heaved his bulk into the barroom. 'Miles,' he called. 'There you are! Thanks for commandeering the limo! I had to come back in the bus with the technicians and the rest of the cast.'

Grayson waved a hand at him, dismissively. 'Don't give me that crap, Charlie. A good assistant director is a team member, not the team leader. Anyway, I had a call coming in from my agent, and I had to be back here to take it.'

The fat man ambled over to our table. 'Too bad. You missed the excitement.'

'Excitement! Up here?'

'Yes. We had a visit from the law. The local crimebusters.'

'What, looking for work as extras?'

'No. Looking for that young lady you're sweet on.'

Beside me, Prim sat bolt upright. Grayson glanced round at her, briefly. 'Did they say what they wanted?' he asked.

The director shook his head. 'They muttered something about her being a witness in a court case. Nothing serious, they said. I told them, "In that case, come back on Monday." That seemed to satisfy them.

'Look, old boy. I'm off for a bath. I'll see you down here

109

for a drink before dinner. Seven-thirty okay?'

'Yes, fine,' Grayson muttered, absently. The fat man nodded, a farewell and slouched out of the room.

'A court case,' said the actor, looking curiously at Prim. 'What d'you think that's about?'

'I told you,' she said, batting not an eyelid. 'I'm just back from Africa. How would I know?'

'Mm. Yeah, of course. Funny, I had this feeling there was something troubling her, something she wasn't telling me, but I didn't press her. Look, if you do find Dawn over the weekend, tell her that if she does have a problem, old Miles'll fix it for her.'

Prim nodded. 'I'll tell her that. I'm sure it'll be nothing, though. Dawn's one of nature's worriers, even when there's absolutely nothing to worry about.' She took my hand again. 'Oz, if Dawn's away till Monday there's no point in hanging about here. If we leave now we can get back home tonight.'

I followed her lead and stood up. 'Okay, let's hit the trail. It's been a pleasure to meet you, Miles. We'll make sure that Dawn's back on Monday, raring to go.'

We started to leave, but I couldn't resist. I'm just a punter at heart, after all. 'I don't suppose you'd autograph a beer mat, would you?' I asked. 'For my Dad, like.'

Grayson laughed, as if reassured that life really did hold no surprises. He took a pen from his breast pocket and scrawled a signature on a Foster's mat. 'Cheers,' I said. 'I'll buy the beer next time.'

'Hold you to that. So long.'

We waved him goodbye and made our way out of the bar, leaving him draining his Fosters.

'What a nice guy,' said Prim.

'Aye, and he fancies your sister too. She could be all right

110

there, if we can just keep her out of the slammer.'

She flashed me a worried smile.

'Are we really going back to Edinburgh?' she asked.

'No thank you very much. I don't think we want to do that right now. Eventually Mike Dylan will have been through every grocer's till in town, and he'll realise we told young Morrow a porky about the fiver. I think we should body-swerve him for now, till we find Dawn. And to be on the safe side we should get out of here too, in case the plods come back looking for *us*.

'Tell you what, it's been a few weeks since I've seen my Dad. We can make it to Anstruther as easily as Edinburgh. Let's head for there, unless you want to go to Auchterarder.'

She shook her head. 'No, I need more time to think up a cover story about Dawn. Let's go to Fife: I fancy meeting the old man who could spawn a son like you!'

In which we dine in style
and Mac the Dentist
is caught *in flagrante*.

I have this thing about drinking and driving, so I let Prim drive us eastward, retracing our route as far as Lochearnhead, where we followed the Perth road, along the lochside, rather than heading for Stirling. The sun was low in the sky as we left the M90 at Milnathort and cruised around Loch Leven, into Fife.

It's a funny place, the old Kingdom, my birthplace; a real amalgam of cultures, with its agriculture in the north, its Black Country to the west, and away on its tip, jutting into the sea, its East Neuk.

'I suppose that the place where you grow up always seems different from anywhere else,' I said to Prim as she drove, quickly but with assurance, 'but every time I go back to the East Neuk now, to Anstruther, I feel like I'm stepping into fairyland. Life has a different pace there, as if time passes more slowly. I don't know another place like it.'

'I know what you mean. When I was wee, and when Dawn was a baby, we went to Elie for our holidays. We took a house

113

for a month. I remember days on the beach, whatever the weather, and scones and Coca Cola in the tennis pavilion. My Granny came with us; she used to sit all afternoon by the bowling green, watching the play. She didn't understand what was going on, but that didn't matter. It was her thing, and she did it.

'I have this secret dream that one day I'll live in Elie.'

I frowned and tutted. 'Us East Neukers don't really approve of Elie. "Elie for the elite", we say. Too many of the houses belong to weekenders. My Dad says that when he was a kid, Elie was a working village. It had fishermen, golf-club makers, market gardeners and so on, and everyone let rooms in their houses to holidaymakers. But then more and more of the houses were bought up by folk from Glasgow and Edinburgh, lawyers and doctors and the like. All of a sudden the place was a ghost town in the winter, and there were fewer holidaymakers in the summer too, as those houses weren't let out any more.

'Now the second and third generations of weekenders are there. Yuppies, most of them are.'

Prim laughed as my mouth curled with distaste. 'Intolerant bugger, aren't you. I'll bet that in Anstruther, they think you're a Yuppie too!' I looked at her in mock horror. 'No. I'm Mac the Dentist's son, him that works in Edinburgh. Jan More, she's the teachers' lassie, her that used tae hang about wi' Mac the Dentist's son. In Enster, there's no way any of us can get too big for our Wellies.'

'No,' she said, almost involuntarily. 'Otherwise there wouldn't be room for the sheep.' I looked at her astonished, but she stayed poker-faced and went on. 'Do Jan's parents still live there?'

'Her Mother does. Her Father, fool that he was, traded her

in for a younger model years ago. Lives in the West some-where. Jan never sees him.'

Prim glanced at me, as she took a corner. 'You and Jan. It is "used to", isn't it?'

'It is now. Jan and I have known each other since we were in our prams. We were best pals when we were kids. As we grew up, things happened between us almost automatically. Everybody in Enster – that's Fifer-speak for Anstruther by the way – everyone assumed we'd get married, and I supposed that we did too for a while. But eventually, once we hit our twenties, we realised that we weren't meant for that. We weren't on fire for each other. So ever since then we've settled for being the best of pals, and occasional lovers. We'll go on being the best of pals.'

Prim nodded. 'Good. I like her. Is there anyone else in her life?'

'There sure is, as you'll find out in time.'

'Oooh. Mysterious, is he. I'll look forward to meeting him.'

The cloak of night was sweeping across the fields as we drove the last few miles, through Colinsburgh, and into Pittenweem. We were both starving, and since Pittenweem's fish and chip shop is legendary far beyond Fife, we stopped there to pick up supper, and extra chips for my Dad.

The lumpy brown paper parcel was hot in my lap as we swung into Anstruther and pulled into the drive. Dad's house faces out to sea, and his surgery is built on to the back, so that the patients don't have to trail through the hall spitting blood on the lino, or worse, on the carpet. Once upon a time that's how it was, until my Mum put her foot down, and made him move his business out back.

We parked at the side of the house and walked round to the front. The moon was up, turning the cold, blue river mouth to silver. We stopped and looked across Dad's immaculate garden, and out to sea. 'This is lovely, Oz,' said Prim. 'And you grew up here.'

'Yup. My Dad would say I'm still growing up.'

I looked up at the big bay window of my Dad's living room. The curtains hadn't been pulled – they never were – and the blueish glow of the television shone in the dark. In the window above, my Dad's bedroom, a light shone.

I have my own key, but when I turned it in the Yale and pushed the front door, it was stopped by a chain. 'Dad,' I shouted. 'It's me. Come and undo this thing. The fish suppers are getting cold.' There was no immediate response, and so I rang the bell. Eventually, a muffled cursing sounded from behind the door and the hall light was switched on.

'For fuck's sake Oz, you might have let me know!' My Father's voice came from behind the door as he fiddled with the chain. After a few seconds, the door swung open wide, and my Dad, Mac the Dentist, stood there, in his big, old dressing gown. His jaw dropped as he saw us, me holding the fish suppers and Prim lugging our travel bag.

'Sorry, Dad,' I said. 'I never thought. Anyway, you know me, I like surprises. And this one's a cracker. Dad, this is my new friend, Primavera Phillips. Prim, this is the man you wanted to meet, Macintosh Blackstone, LDS, the bugger who christened me Osbert!'

My Dad shook his head. 'Jesus, I don't know. Come in and welcome, lassie. I don't know what you've done to deserve this guy for company, but I'll do my best to see that he behaves himself.

'As far as surprises go, Oz my boy, two of us can play that game.'

In all my life, I've never managed to put one over on my

Father. He is absolutely the most resourceful, wise, devious, cunning and artful old bastard that I know.

We stepped into the hall and it was my turn for the dropping jaw. I saw her feet first as she came down the stairs, then black slacks, then a colourful blouse, and finally . . . 'Auntie Mary!'

Mary More, Jan's Mother, has been an honorary aunt all my days, except at primary school when I had to call her 'Miss' like all the rest of the teachers. For all that she is fifty-three, she is still a slim, handsome woman, and, according to her daughter, a walking testimonial to the benefits of hormone replacement therapy.

She smiled, and tossed her carefully maintained auburn chest. 'Hello Oz. Are you still playing detectives or is this a pure accident?'

'Accident, Mary, honest. If I'd known, I'd have . . .'

'What,' said my Dad, 'stayed away? Don't be daft. Drop that bag and get through to the kitchen. There'll be no fish suppers in my living room. Hope you've got some chips for us. Primavera . . . lovely name . . . would you like tea or coffee, or something else?'

Auntie Mary took charge. 'Mac. Upstairs and get yourself dressed. I'll take care of the tea or whatever. What will it be, my dear?'

She looked at Prim with a friendly, enquiring smile, but hidden in there I caught a line of communication, an inflection in her gaze. I know that she wouldn't have meant to let it show, but I caught it clearly. It told me that I had just snapped the last faint thread between Mary and an unspoken wish, one that I never dreamt was there, that eventually Jan and I *would* be a couple, that we would toe the line and become a conventional pair of thirty-somethings, with a house in an acceptable suburb, a decent car in the garage and two point four cats or whatever. Poor Mary; if I'd only known, I could have told her long ago. Jan did tell her, but now it was clear that she never quite believed it.

But the look passed. Prim glanced across at me, and I rescued her. 'I think what we really need is to raid the fridge, Mary. Unless that old bugger's finished the Becks' I left here last time.'

She laughed. 'No chance of that. You know how your Dad feels about beer that doesn't come in pints.' She turned again to Prim. 'We haven't been introduced, dear. I'm Mary More. Don't let the "Auntie" stuff give you awful ideas about Mac and me. "Friend of the family" is how I am best described.

'How long have you known young Osbert here?'

I held my breath. Prim grinned and shrugged her shoulders. 'Who knows? The moment I met him it was as if he'd always been there.'

'That's it then,' said Mary. 'Just make sure you always are, Oz.' She led the way into the kitchen, and reached into the cupboard above one of the kitchen worksurfaces, to produce two white dinner plates. I noticed that she knew exactly where to look.

Prim unwrapped the fish suppers and loaded one on to each plate, while I knocked the tops off of two cold Becks'. I held one out to Mary, but she shook her head. 'No thanks Oz, I must be off home.'

'Don't be daft, Mary. Just because we're here . . .'

Her eyebrows arched, in much the same way they had when someone spoke in class. 'As if I would bother about that! Oh no, you don't think I stay over do you? Remember where you are. This is Anstruther. The first time my bedroom light doesn't go on after *News At Ten* the jungle drums will be sounding all over town.' My Dad appeared, as she spoke, in the kitchen doorway, looking reasonably tidy in a crew-neck sweater and grey trousers. Too bad about the trainers, though. 'Isn't that right, Mac?'

'Oh aye. Ps and Qs must be watched. I think they're on to us though. We went along to Elie for a meal in the Ship a few weeks back. One of my patients was in. Ever since then I've been getting funny looks in the paper shop.' He took Mary's hand. 'Come on, hen. Let's be daring. I'll walk you home.'

'Indeed you will not! Besides, you've got your chips to finish. Goodnight both.' A wave and she was gone. Dad was allowed to see her to the back door, her shortcut home, and then he was back, plopping himself beside us at the big, pine kitchen table and wolfing his chips straight from the paper.

'Well,' he said, between mouthfuls, as we tore into the Pittenweem haddock, 'what brought you two up here unannounced, interrupting my Friday night tryst?'

I swallowed some of my Becks', from the bottle. I'm not a poser, honest. It really is the best way to drink it. 'Spur of the moment, really, Dad. We just decided it was time for you to meet Prim.'

'Mmm. And delighted I am too. You've been sharing your life with a fucking lizard for far too long!'

He looked across at Primavera. 'Pardon the barrackroom talk, my dear. It's the way we are, Osbert and I. We used the word to give emphasis to a point.'

Prim, resting from her attack on the fish and chips, propped both elbows on the table and took her beer in both hands. 'That's all right, Mr Blackstone. I've been in barrackrooms, in Africa. You should hear, and see, how those boys emphasise their points.'

Dad smiled. 'I can see you're going to fit in around here. There's one thing though. To everyone but that insolent bugger

119

there, my name is Mac. Fair enough?'

She nodded. 'Fair enough.'

We went back to our fish suppers, but before the end, I realised that I was flagging. I looked across at Prim, and I could see that she was drooping too. I glanced at my watch. It was 10.30 p.m. We had been flying, with precious little sleep, for thirty-six hours. Now the tanks were empty and we were both ready to crash.

She caught my glance, and looked at Dad. 'Mac, would you mind if I had a bath and went to bed?'

'Not at all, the pair of you look as if you've got a fair few miles on your clocks. Oz, show the lady where we keep the zinc bath.'

My room looks out across the Firth too. It used to be Ellen's, by right of primogeniture (there's a big word for a simple boy), but as soon as she left home for good I moved myself in there. I held Prim, in the dark, and we looked out of the window across the river. Night had fallen completely now and we could see the lights on May Island, closest to us this time, across on the Bass Rock and further along on Fidra, as each lanced its different signal into the night.

'D'you want to watch the sun come up again?'

She turned and kissed me, her lips tasting richly of salt and vinegar. 'No, my dear, I want to sleep till around midday, if that's all right with you.'

'Sleep as long as you like, as long as you don't waken me.'

'There's no danger of that,' she whispered, kissing me again, and smiling. 'Because you'll be next door.'

I put yet another gallant proposition to her, but she silenced me with a finger on my lips. 'Oz, you're too knackered to do me justice.' I had to admit it: she was right.

I checked to make sure that there was a sheet on the bed

under the duvet. There was, and the pillow slips were crisp and fresh. 'You sleep here, then,' I said. 'Have your bath, and I'll go down and crack another beer with the old man. He's dreaming if he thinks he's going to get away without being interrogated about Auntie Mary!'

I produced a couple of big, fluffy towels and my spare dressing gown from the hall cupboard, and showed her where the bathroom was, at the end of the landing. The bath was huge and deep and had been there since the house was built. When I was really wee, I could swim in it. There was even some scented stuff, for making bubbles. I leaned over to twist on the brass taps. By the time I straightened up and turned around Prim was half undressed. Her shirt was on the floor, her skirt was unfastened, and her bra hung from her shoulders, loose and unclipped.

Her erect nipples, showing clearly through the lace fabric, tilted slightly upwards; they caught and held me like a burglar in a searchlight. I reached for her. She smiled, and put her hands on my chest. 'I know bravado when I see it, my man. Go and have that beer. I'll leave the water in the bath. From the size of this thing, even half-full it'll drain the tank.'

I nodded, kissed her, said farewell to her glorious head-lamps and went back downstairs. My Dad was still in the kitchen, finishing the chips that we had left. I uncapped another bottle and we went through to the living room, where he poured himself a whisky. A very small whisky, I was pleased to see.

He slumped into his chair, facing the window, and I sprawled on the couch. There were no lamps on, and since it was early summer, the fire was unlit. Dad and I like to sit in the moonlight. A pair of lunatics, he says.

He sipped his malt. 'I like your lady, Oz. She's for you. How long have you known her?'

I smiled in the shadows. 'If I tell you, you'll really think I'm daft.'

'Always have, always will. Come on.'

'Okay then. I met her yesterday morning. Go on then, laugh.'

But he didn't. His domed grey head slumped, and his wise eyes stared into the hearth, at the fire screen that my Mum embroidered the year before she died, as if he was looking into the past . . . as he was.

'Son,' . . . he only ever calls me that when he's being deadly serious . . . 'the day I met your mother, I said to myself, "I'm going to marry her." The next day, I said it to her. She said, "All right, now that's sorted out let's take some time to get to know each other." I'm not going to laugh at you, boy, because I've been there. Good luck to you both.'

He looked across at me and I saw his eyes glisten.

'Thanks, Dad.' I didn't have anything more to say.

He did. 'One thing, though. Your moments haven't had spurs on them since you were about fourteen. What's brought you tearing up here when by rights you should still be shacked up in that loft of yours?'

I shook my head. 'Tomorrow, Dad, tomorrow.

'Anyway, enough about me. What's with you and Auntie Mary then? I knew you'd been seeing a bit of each other, but I didn't realise how much. How long's this been going on?'

'About a year.'

'Is it serious?'

'What's serious when you're fifty-eight? Sure, the old loins still catch fire from time to time, but the difference is that you're less likely to go hunting for the matches. No, pal, by that time your preoccupation is with the prospect of going into old age alone.

'Mary and I have known each other for donkey's years. Truth be told, I've cast an eye over her for most of that time, but while your mother was alive, and Alex More was around there was never any thought, on either side, of any . . . any, misbehaving.

'Things have changed now. We're both single, for different reasons. After a while, well, it just happened. Now, I think Mary's happy enough, and she sure keeps me on the straight and narrow. Her basket would be full if Jan . . . but I suppose not.'

I shook my head. 'Not much chance of that, Dad, I don't think.'

'No? Ach well . . .'

'Does Jan know about . . . ?' I asked, hesitantly.

'No. If she did, d'you think she'd have said nothing to you?'

I shook my head. 'D'you think you'll get married?'

He looked at me, frankly. 'If we do, you'll be the first to know. But come on, boy, don't sit here any longer. Get away upstairs before that lass forgets what you look like.'

'Come on, Dad. We're not at that stage yet.' I pushed myself out of my chair. 'I am off to bed, though. See you after your surgery. Maybe we'll hit a few balls, eh. I'll see what Prim says.' A wonderful thought struck me. 'Hey, maybe she plays golf!'

I saw the light still shining under the bathroom door as I reached the top of the stairs. I tapped the door and Prim opened it, swathed in one of the towels. Her hair was hand-dried and stood up in spikes. Her face was scrubbed shiny; without a trace of make-up her eyes seemed even bigger, her lips fuller. I thought she was the loveliest thing I'd ever seen in my life. Come to think of it, I still do.

She smiled at me and pulled me into the bathroom. She'd

123

been as good as her word. The bubbles were clearing, but the bath was still steaming gently. 'In you go, if you want. I'll still be awake, if you want to say goodnight.' She stood in the doorway, smiling.

'The water's okay, is it?' I said. 'You didn't pee in it or anything?'

She giggled. 'Of course I did! But you love me, don't you?' She pulled the door closed behind her.

Her body was still hot from the tub, like mine, when I slipped into my room and sat on the edge of the bed. I stroked her cheek as she lay on the pillow. 'Do you want me to pull the curtains?' I asked her.

'No,' she said, drowsily. I kissed her forehead, and as I did I looked into her heavy eyes, and felt sleep begin to take me too. 'Goodnight, then,' I whispered in her ear. 'Oh yes. I almost forgot to ask. Do you play golf?'

In which we play seventeen holes and the Jag stays on the road.

She does, of course. Pretty well too. We were lucky to get a threesome off at Elie on a Saturday afternoon, but my Dad's been a member there since God was a boy.

Elie Golf House Club has to be the only course in the world with a submarine periscope built into its starter's hut. No. I'm not joking. A submarine periscope.

We were waved off, and my Dad clumped an awkward drive halfway up the face of the hill, 100 yards in front of the first tee, which makes the contraption necessary. Prim and I, sharing my clubs – the Nissan's boot serves as a locker for all my sports gear – clipped our shots safely over the direction post, and we were off.

The quirky old course, spread out on its three fields, unfolded itself for us in the afternoon sun. Our golf was pure mince but we didn't care. It was a nice afternoon, if a bit windy, and Prim and my Dad got on like a house on fire. Eventually, like many an Elie golfer, we decided to skip the eighteenth hole and go straight to the nineteenth. The old Golf

Tavern has changed less, probably than any pub I know. My Dad still calls it 'Elrick's', although that licensee has been gone from it since I was a child.

I got them in, and we sat at a table in the window, crunching crisps and playing dominoes.

'So what's this story,' said my Dad, slamming down the double five, 'that you were going to tell me? What brought you up here?'

I looked at Prim. She nodded.

'Okay, but we better finish the dominoes, 'cause it'll put you right off your game.'

'Nonsense. You could poke me in both eyes with a sharp stick and you still couldn't beat me at Doms. Come on, tell me your story.'

'If you insist. After you've got them in.'

He shook his head. 'My God! Does everything have a price?' He stood up and took the single step across to the high bar counter. He was no sooner back with two pints of Deuchars and a small whisky for him than the door creaked open. The Golf Tavern is a great place for old bodgers. This one had a dog, a great, fat, slavering labrador. It was the sort of dog you find at one time or another in every country pub, its function being to see its master home in time for supper.

The old bodger turned out to be a patient. 'Hello Mac,' he hailed, the red capillaries standing out on his nose. 'Don't see you along here very often. Glad I bumped into you. Had this terrible bloody ache for a week now.' He hauled his loose lips wide apart to reveal a yellow canine of which the lab would have been ashamed. Half an hour and two more dog walkers later, we made it back to Dad's elderly Jag, parked outside the clubhouse. 'Jesus!' he spluttered, as he eased himself behind the big dish of the steering wheel. 'No wonder I don't come along here too often. One of them in there actually asked me to look at his fucking dog! Did you hear him?'

He shoved the lever into Drive and eased smoothly out of the car park, up through Elie, past the grey church, and out of the village. 'Right,' he said as Prim, in the back seat, pointed to the jagged shape of the Lady's Tower, 'let's have your story.'

And so I told him. Everything. From the moment when I found the late Willie Kane, to the time when we interrupted his coitus. The only part that I left out was my flash of insight about the identity of the killer. I didn't think Prim was ready for that.

I was about eight when I found out what 'phlegmatic' meant. 'It's what your father is,' said my Mum, and I understood. The Jag only looked like swerving off the road once, when I told him about meeting Miles Grayson in the Falls of Lora. 'Did you get his autograph?' asked the old movie buff.

'As a matter of fact I did.' I smiled at Prim. 'Bet you thought I was kidding when I said it was for my Dad.'

He was silent for the rest of the drive home. I knew better than to interrupt him. Mac the Dentist is a great ponderer. When he's come to a view he'll share it with the world, but while it's hatching in his brain, best to leave him alone.

We didn't go back into the house at once. Instead Dad motioned us over to his long green garden seat, positioned at the top of the lawn. We sat down, Prim between us. There was a big black tanker making its way out to sea, riding low in the water with its cargo of oil. He pointed to it. 'See that thing? When I was a young man, if anyone had told me that one day we'd be exporting oil from this river, I'd have told him he was off his fucking head. Now we take it for granted. But when it's all gone, we'll miss it.' He sat silent for a minute or so longer, then dug Prim in the ribs. 'You still got that fiver then?'

'Yes.'

'And you, boy. You don't trust this man Archer, do you?' I hadn't told him that.

'If I were you, I'd go back to see him one more time. Tell him you think Prim's sister has the fiver, and that you're looking for her. See how he reacts, then decide what to do.'

'What are my choices?'

He raised an eyebrow. 'Say "Bugger it", give up on the reward, go to the police, tell them the whole story and give them the fiver. That's what a sensible man would have done by now. Or, come clean with Archer, go and collect his dough, and take your cut. Or, and daftest of all, keep it to yourself, and once you've found Prim's sister and covered her backside, go to Switzerland, pick up the money and then make up your mind what to do with it.'

'And what would you do?'

'I, oh Mighty Oz? What would I do?' His face creased into a sly grin. 'I've never been accused of being too sensible, have I!'

He jumped to his feet. 'Come on, you two. The day presses on, and we have a date. Mary phoned this morning while you were still out of it, and bade us all to dinner at her place.'

In which Mac the Dentist
gives us some good advice,
and I become a lighthouse keeper.

It had been years since I'd dined at Auntie Mary's, and then I'd been too much of an airhead to appreciate what a wonderful cook she is. We ate salmon terrine that she'd made herself, braised venison from an estate a few miles away, garnished with peas straight from the pod, carrots and new potatoes, all home-grown, and a huge pineapple, quartered and soaked in Benedictine. Fortunately we'd taken a couple of decent bottles of wine with us, not Dad's usual supermarket crap. That would have tasted like vinegar alongside Mary's gourmet meal.

The table talk avoided relationships. Instead Prim told us tales of Africa, I told us tales of accidental comedy among my witness interviews, and Dad told us tales of dental dereliction. I watched him as the evening went on. The old bugger had his feet under the table, no doubt about that.

Auntie Mary brought out the port with the coffee and truffles. Damn good stuff it was too. Dad took to it, for sure. After his second glass he was clearly on his way. I wasn't worried about a slide back to the bottle. Before Mum died, he had always enjoyed a good bevvy as a form of fellowship. He had been a happy drunk, one who used alcohol to enhance enjoyment rather than drive away worries. It was funny, but looking at him across the table, I was actually pleased to see him getting pleasantly pissed. It was just like old times. Mary might as well have been my Mum, except, although I feel disloyal in admitting this, she's a better cook.

At last the port bottle was down to only the dregs. Dad toyed with the idea of finishing it, but thought better of it. He muttered something about the eye of a needle at thirty paces and put the bottle down. Suddenly he leaned across the table and took Prim's hand. 'Tell me, my dear,' he said, heavy-lidded. 'What are you going to do t'morrow?'

Prim looked at him, smiling lightly, her cheeks slightly red from the port. 'What do you think I should do, Mac?'

'I think you should go and see your Mum.'

The smile left her lips. She frowned uncertainly.

'Listen, love,' said my wise old father. 'You owe it to her. It's her right to worry about her daughter; goes with the position of parent. If there's cause for her to be anxious, she won't thank you for keeping it from her. Most of us old yins are capable of facing up to life, you know, whatever it throws at us.'

She looked at him for a while, and the smile came back. 'You're right, aren't you. I was treating her as if she was in her dotage. Okay, tomorrow we're off to Auchterarder. Apart from anything else, it's time she found out what her older daughter's up to!'

Dad nodded, and rattled the port bottle again. I took my cue, and stood up. 'Mary, that was wonderful, but it's time we were off.' Prim stood up and took my hand as I stepped round the table.

'Coming, Dad?' I said.

'No, no. Think I'll hang on here for a wee while.' He glanced across at Auntie Mary. She answered his slightly raised eyebrow with a nod.

The door was almost closed when he called after me. 'Tell you what, Oz. Be a good lad and put my bedroom light on for a wee while. Just to keep the neighbours happy, you understand.'

It might have been no more than the creaking of a chair, but as I closed the door, I was sure that I heard him fart.

In which we find she who wasn't lost at all, in which I experience the full glory of a Scottish Sabbath, from which we make an escape, and in which something very unpleasant happens.

To me, Auchterarder isn't a place at all. It's a stagecoach halt that's managed somehow to carry itself over into the twentieth century. It's something of a dormitory town, I suppose, but its main purpose today seems to be to meet the needs of Gleneagles Hotel, the fat cat up the road; to keep its kitchens filled; to make sure that its golf courses are all in the mint condition that its American and Japanese patrons have been told to expect; to ensure that there's always a taxi available to run same to and from Glasgow and Edinburgh Airports. Other than that, there isn't a logical reason for its existence.

Except of course that it's where Primavera Phillips was raised to womanhood. That makes it special.

We drove up the motorway in midmorning – having left a 'Thanks and see you later,' note on the kitchen table for my still-absent Dad – and took the fast road down from Perth.

'Our house is on the edge of the town,' said Prim as we took the turnoff from the A9. 'It's a big barn of a place up on the right.'

That was far short of a reasonable description. It struck me at first when I saw it that if it had had the Bates Motel at the foot of the garden, it could have been lifted straight out of *Psycho*. Closer to, I realised that I should have been thinking of the Addams Family. The Phillips homestead is a big spacious villa, with two high storeys and an attic, and a steep roof that must have been a slater's nightmare when it was built.

'There you are. Semple House. What d'you think?' said Prim, smiling, biting her lip, as the Nissan's tyres scrunched up the red gravel path.

'You don't have a butler called Lurch, do you?'

'Swine!' she shouted, laughing, and punched my arm. We eased ourselves out of the car and trotted up the six steps to the front door. Prim fumbled in her handbag for her keys. Eventually she found the bunch and fiddled through it for the right one.

She needn't have bothered. The door swung open . . . with an authentic Addams Mansion creak, I was glad to note. Prim looked up, and gasped.

They aren't instantly alike. They're both gorgeous, but in very different ways. Dawn Phillips is dark, while Prim is authentically blonde, even when her hair isn't bleached by the sun. Dawn's natural expression, the one with which right there and then I guessed she opens every door, is one of apprehension, while Prim's is one of total confidence, welcoming whatever challenge the world has to offer. But there is something about their eyes, about the tilt of the nose, which marks them out as sisters, beyond a shadow of a doubt.

They stood there like statues, on their parents' doorstep, staring at each other, their mouths hanging open. It struck me that it was like watching someone looking in a distorted mirror.

Dawn cracked first. Her eyes filled with tears. 'Prim! Oh God, you're safe. We've been so worried about you, out there with all that trouble going on. When did you get back?' She stepped out from the doorway and hugged her sister.

'Hey, girl,' said Prim, disengaging and holding her at arm's length. 'Didn't I write? Didn't I phone when I could? Didn't I call Mum on Friday to say I was home?'

Dawn shook her head. 'I didn't know. I went up to Perth on Friday to chill out with Jenny Brown and get pissed. I've been so screwed up lately. I only got back half an hour ago.'

'Before Friday, how long had you been here?'

Dawn jumped when I spoke. She was edgy, and no mistake. Prim smiled, and took my arm. 'Sorry, I should have done the introductions first. This is Oz; Oz Blackstone, my new friend.'

The young Miss Phillips looked me up and down. My jeans had seen better days, but haven't everyone's, and at least my white tee-shirt was clean and my trainers didn't smell. Eventually she held out a hand. 'Pleased to meet you, Oz. Did she bring you back from Africa?'

I shook my head, and her hand. 'No. Anstruther, in fact. And before that, from Connell. We've been looking all around Scotland for you.'

She frowned, looking genuinely puzzled. 'But . . .'

Prim cut her off, shooing her inside the house and pulling me in after her. 'We'll get to that in a minute, Dawn,' she said, carefully. 'First of all let's get the kettle on. Where are Mum and Dad?'

'It's Sunday. They've gone to church.' '*Mmm*,' I thought. '*People still do that, do they*!'

It was a nice old house on the inside. Full of character. It seemed that the Phillips family hadn't thrown anything away for about three generations. As I looked around the hall, I had a funny feeling that I couldn't pin down for a moment or two. Eventually it came to me. 'It's like stepping back into my Granny Blackstone's house.' I spoke the thought aloud.

'Yes, sort of old-fashioned comfy, isn't it,' said Prim. 'My Dad likes old things.' She pointed me into a big living room, off the hall, and disappeared with Dawn in another direction. I looked around the room. It was dominated by a huge brown three-piece suite in leather and velvet, and the pleasant smell of the hide hung in the air. Everything else – curtains, rugs, furniture, huge wooden-framed radio – was of the same 1930s vintage. A telly would have seemed obscene in there.

'It's a museum, isn't it,' said Prim, from the doorway, behind me. 'Lovely to visit, but not to live in. Not for me, anyway.

'Sit down,' she ordered. 'Dawn's making the tea.' She flopped on to the big sofa, pulling me down beside her. The big velvet cushions whooshed up around me with my weight. I've never laid on a feather-bed, but when I do, I imagine it'll feel like the Phillips family settee. Prim curled up on her cushion, sitting with her legs pulled up like she does in the car. She was wearing a white sleeveless wool top and pale blue shorts. The way she was sitting I could see her knickers. Suddenly my jeans felt tighter as old Mr Stiffy began to make his presence felt. I reached out for her, but she jumped up, a smile on her delicious lips. 'Oz! It's Sunday. My folks are Sabbatarians. No radio on Sunday, no playing cards, and absolutely no nooky on the living-room carpet!

'Besides, this is serious. What are we going to tell Dawn?'

Dragged back to reality, I shook my head. 'We're going to ask her a few things first. She . . .'

'Ask me?' Dawn was in the doorway carrying teapot, cups and saucers on a big tray with folding legs. 'Ask me what?'

136

'How you came to be in a movie, for a start,' said Prim, quickly.

'Oh,' said Dawn. 'All that hasn't really sunk in yet. It was pure luck. There was a part for an actress and Miles wanted someone Scottish. He came to the Lyceum one night when I was on and saw me. Next day, I had a note from the director asking me to come for a test.'

'That's great. How's it going?'

'Terrific, so far. I was supposed to be ravished and killed by the Redcoats quite early on, but Miles has given me a reprieve. They've written some more scenes for me and I'm getting supporting billing. A bit more money too.'

'You seem to be doing all right in other ways,' I chipped in. 'We met Miles. He fancies you, and no mistake.'

Dawn glanced at me as she poured the tea and smiled self-consciously, nervily. I could see that, temperamentally, she was her sister's opposite.

'So,' said Prim, 'with all that's going for you, how come you're screwed up. What's with the Prozac?'

'Oh it's lots of things, but mostly, as usual, it's men. I've got myself trapped in a sort of, situation, and I was having trouble finding a way out.' '*Christ,*' I thought, '*if that was her solution I found in Prim's flat it was a bit drastic.*'

'I was having stage fright, quite badly. The Prozac sorted it out, but it didn't do anything for the root cause of the trouble.' '*No?*' I thought again. '*Maybe it took the kitchen knife to sort that out.*'

'Remember the guy I told you about in a letter?'

'Danny deVito meets Nijinski?' said Prim.

'Yes, that's right. His name's William Kane. He's a regular at the theatre. His firm are corporate sponsors. I met him at our theatre club one night. We got talking, and I thought he

137

was sort of funny, but sad at the same time. He was carrying a burden, I could tell.'

Prim sighed. 'Aah. Another bloody bird with a broken wing! I thought you'd grown out of that.'

'You don't though, do you. At least I don't. Anyway Willie isn't like that. He isn't helpless or anything. He phoned me a couple of days after the reception and asked me out. He came to the play, then took me to dinner, and it was fun. We did it again, and soon it was a regular thing.'

'He's married of course, Dawn, isn't he?' There was an edge of disapproval in Prim's voice. Her sister's cheeks flushed, quickly. She nodded.

'Yes,' she said quietly. 'Look, I know this'll sound awful, but his marriage is a sham. He and his wife are around forty; they've been married unhappily for years. She's unfaithful to him, and she doesn't hide it. In fact she rubs Willie's nose in it. She has a relationship with someone she was at school with.' Prim shot me a raised-eyebrow glance. 'They were boy and girl school captains at the same time, but afterwards they went their separate ways, until they met up again a couple of years ago.

'The way things were, I didn't feel uncomfortable about sleeping with Willie.' She grinned, suddenly with a strange, mischievous look in her eyes. 'Except . . .' She flushed again and glanced at me.

'Yes?' said Prim.

'Tell you later,' she said, looking meaningfully in my direction once more. '*You nearly let on about Willie's big Willy, didn't you*.' I was bursting to say it, but I resisted. 'Let's just say there was a physical problem,' she added. I coughed on a sip of tea. Prim shot me a '*Shurrup*' look.

'It was fun at first,' Dawn went on. 'But Willie's obsessive.

138

Pretty soon he was telling me he loved me and everything. That made me nervous, but I thought it'd wear off. It didn't though. One day he turned up on the doorstep of your flat with a suitcase. He said he'd left Linda and was moving in with me. I didn't know what to do. I mean if I'd chucked him out he'd have had nowhere else to go, but . . . well, to tell you the truth, nice as he is, when we got down to it I found out pretty soon that physically, I don't really fancy him.'

'Bloody great,' said Prim. 'The guy turned you off, but you let him shack up with you. And in my flat. A bit of a bloody nerve that, wasn't it? Having it off with another woman's husband in my flat. Private eyes at the door and all that.'

'Oh come on,' said Dawn, defensively. 'His wife wouldn't do that.'

Prim shot me another '*Shurrup*,' look, but I decided that it was time to get into the discussion. 'When was the last time you saw him?' I asked, as casually as I could.

She looked blankly at me. 'A couple of weeks ago,' she said. 'I left him in Ebeneezer Street when I went off filming. I told him he'd have to find somewhere permanent to live. I didn't *say* I wouldn't be coming with him, but I tried not to make him think that I would.

'He just said not to worry, that everything would be sorted out soon.'

'You didn't go back to Edinburgh on Wednesday?'

'No. I came here, to see Mum and Dad. The thing is, I really fancy Miles too, and I want to clear the decks. I thought I'd ask Dad to go to see Willie, to say I want out, and to ask him to be sure to move out of the flat before I got back.'

Prim snorted. 'That'd be really nice of Dad. Have you asked him yet?'

'No, I haven't plucked up the courage. I don't suppose

139

you'd . . .' And then something struck her, something very obvious.

'But hold on. You're back, Prim. So you must have been to the flat. Wasn't Willie there? Have you chucked him out already?'

Primavera shook her head. 'Sit down, Dawn,' she said quietly. Her sister obeyed. 'Yes, I've been to the flat, and yes, I've seen Willie. So has Oz. But he was dead. He was murdered. On Wednesday night, the police say.'

The girl's face went ashen. She hid it with her hands and slumped backwards, collapsing into the soft cushions of the big armchair. I thought that she was crying, but she wasn't. She was too shocked for that. It was Prim who was suddenly in tears. She rushed across the room, and threw her arms round her sister. 'Oh Dawn, I'm sorry, but I'm so relieved. We didn't want to think it, but we were afraid that you might have had something to do with it, or that you might be in danger too. That's why we've been looking for you.'

I felt helpless, so I got up and put my arms around them both. 'It's okay,' I said. 'It's okay, Prim. We've found her now, and she's going to be all right.' I drew her to her feet and held her against me. In the armchair, Dawn took her hands from her ghost's face and looked up at us.

'Do the police know who did it?' she said, huskily.

I shook my head. 'No. The guy in charge is going to want to talk to you. Was Willie in touch with anyone? His wife, for example?'

'Not as far as I know? But I haven't seen him for two weeks, remember.'

'Did he tell you about the money?'

'What money?' Prim and I looked hard at her. She was an actress, but I couldn't imagine that anyone could fake that sort of astonishment.

'Did Willie send you to Switzerland to open a bank account for him?'

She gave a soft gasp. 'Oh, that. Yes. He said he wanted to hide as much of his money from his wife as he could. He said she'd be suspicious if she found out that he'd gone to Switzerland, so he asked me to do it. I flew to Geneva and opened the account, then flew back on the same day.

'The account's in a bank called Berners: it's one of these cloak and dagger things. Withdrawals can only be made by two people, each carrying half of a fiver. The account number is the same as the number on the banknote. The bank took a photo of it. When I got back I gave the two halves to Willie.' She pulled herself up in the chair.

'But why did you ask about money? Did Willie use the account? Did he transfer his cash out there?'

I smiled. 'I don't know about *his* cash, but he transferred nine hundred thousand of his firm's money out there. I was hired by the senior partner to recover it. I went to see him on Thursday, to get the fiver back. He was dead when I got there, and when Prim arrived. That's when we met.

'We've been a bit busy since then,' I added.

Dawn sat there staring up at us as she fitted the pieces of the story together. By now I was quite certain that Prim's sister was just a touch slow on the uptake, but eventually she got there. 'Do the police think I killed Willie for the money?'

'The guy who's leading the investigation, Mike Dylan, he doesn't know about the money. And that's the way I want it to stay. Black and Muirton want to keep that part of it quiet. But if Dylan ever does find out about it, and about you opening that bank account, then yes, he'd fancy you for it right away. So let's hope you can prove where you were when Kane was

141

killed.' Dawn gulped. Her mouth dropped open slightly. Prim looked at her anxiously.

'So,' she said, 'when did you get here on Wednesday?'

'About two-thirty in the afternoon.'

'And were you with Mum and Dad all day after that?'

'Yes. Dad had an order to dispatch that day for a customer in London. I helped him box it, then we went to the station in Perth and put it on a train. That would have been around nine in the evening.' She paused. 'Hey, I signed the dispatch slip, and it has the time on it!' Her face lit up with relief.

'After that we came back home and had supper with Mum. I told them all about the film. We sat up until about one in the morning.'

It was my turn to grin with relief. I mean, you don't fancy even the outside possibility that your girlfriend's sister might be a knife-wielding maniac, do you? 'Dawn, that's brilliant,' I said. 'Dylan won't be able to lay a glove on you.'

'Should I go to the police?'

'I don't know. Let's think about that one for a while.

'One thing though. Just remember, if and when you do see Mike Dylan, don't mention a word to him about the bank account. If he should ask you about it, look blank, then tell us.'

She nodded. 'Okay. What about the fiver? Who's got that?'

I looked at Prim. Prim looked at me, and shook her head, imperceptibly. 'The important thing, Dawn,' I said, 'is that whoever killed Willie *doesn't* have it. They couldn't find it at the time, but they sure as hell want it now.' I thought some more, and as I did, there was a loud creak from the hallway. Prim drew a finger across her throat in a 'Keep your mouth shut!' sign, then rubbed her face quickly with her hands to clear away the traces of her earlier tears.

Looking at Mum and Dad Phillips in their churchgoing

clothes, I had a sudden strange feeling that Prim, Dawn and I, the three of us, were time travellers, who had taken a flip back sixty years. Mum was dressed in a long brown velvet dress with a fur stole and a funny, shapeless wee hat that sat on top of her head like a cowpat. Dad wore a heavy black suit, with a jacket so long that it was almost a frock coat. He wore, big round glasses, and a gold watch chain hung across his waistcoat. His high shirt collar was starched stiff, and secured by a brass stud which showed just above the knot of his striped tie. I guessed that he was in his early sixties, his wife maybe five years or so younger. Each was probably around the same age as their clothes.

'Primavera! When we saw the car, we hoped it was you!' Mrs Phillips had a voice like a bell. It rang grandly around the room, and I thought for a second I could hear the glassware tremble. But it had a kind tone, and I knew at once that I was going to like her. Prim rushed across to the doorway and hugged her mother. Behind them, her Dad smiled awkwardly, as if taken aback by such a show of emotion. Then she turned to him, and pulled him to her also, kissing his cheek. I was surprised when his eyes glistened, and so, I think was he. I thought about shedding the odd tear myself, to spare the poor bloke's embarrassment.

Eventually, they noticed that I was there. They couldn't help it. I stood there in my jeans and tee-shirt, fidgeting and feeling as awkward as I ever had in my life. They didn't stare at me, they just looked, as they'd probably look at a deer that wandered into their garden. *'Nice, isn't it?' 'Yes, as long as it doesn't eat the tulips!'* Prim took pity on the alien life-form whom she'd brought into the house. She came across and wrapped herself around me, holding me like a drunk holds a bus-stop, as if he's taking it home to the wife.

'Mum, Dad. This is Oz Blackstone. He's crackers, but I think you'll like him. I do.'

How do you respond to an introduction like that? I came out with, 'Pleased to meet you, after all this time.' The words sort of fell out of my mouth. It was as if they'd been generated by something other than my brain. Without breaking Prim's bearhug, I reached out and shook hands with them both.

Mrs Phillips looked me up and down one more time. 'Well, Oz,' she said, slowly, weightily. 'I've waited a long time to hear my older daughter say something like that, so I'm pleased to meet you too.' She flicked a finger towards Dawn and added, archly. 'That one, of course, says something like that every three months or so, and from the way she was talking on Wednesday, I think we're about to hear it again.'

'That's not all we're going to hear, I hope,' said Mr Phillips, eyeballing his wife meaningfully. He's a dry sort, Prim's father. He looks as if he was made from the wood he carves himself, and he tends to say not much more than one of his toy soldiers. But when he does contribute, it hits the spot.

'All in good time, David,' said Mrs Phillips, 'but first, lunch. Come on, girls.'

'I'll help too,' I said at once, faced with the possibility of being left alone with the totem pole. But it wasn't that easy. 'Not at all, Oz,' said Mother. 'You sit down.' Prim looked back at me, smiling, as she followed her towards the kitchen.

Dad Phillips and I stood there for a few moments, in an awkward silence. And then he coughed, and I realised that he was even less at ease than I was. 'This must be very, er, sudden, for you,' I ventured. 'Both daughters at home more or less out of the blue, and one of them with a bloke in tow.'

He eyed me, checking for any sign that I was humouring

144

him. Then, all at once, he nodded and the ice was broken. 'Yes, you're right. I haven't had much practice at small talk in recent years, not since I sold my factory. Elanore and I each have our own interests, and they tend to be solitary. She writes, I carve wood into interesting shapes and paint it. We don't have many visitors, apart from the occasional girl chums our daughters bring with them. As a matter of fact, you're the first man friend that Primavera's brought here since she was at college.'

I beamed, bursting with pride, until very gently, he pricked my balloon. 'She's always been an individual, has Primavera. Odd tastes in most things.

'What's Oz short for?'

I told him. He nodded, in sympathy, I thought.

'What do you do?'

I told him. 'No divorce work,' I added hastily.

He shrugged. 'No matter. Someone's got to do it. Does it pay well?'

'I'm self-employed. I expect thirty grand net in a reasonable year. Forty in a good one.'

'Mmmm.' There was something in his 'Mmmm' that told me I'd passed my first test.

'D'you play chess?' said Mr Phillips, suddenly.

'I know how the men move,' I said guardedly. One thing more do I know. If anyone over sixty ever offers to take you on at dominoes, darts, chess or squash, be careful: especially if it's squash. There's nothing worse than being humbled at a young person's game by someone who puts his bus pass at the front of the court and adjusts his knee bandages before you begin. I know this from experience.

'That's enough,' he said, a decision made. He walked over to a side window and returned carrying, carefully, a chessboard on a stand. The pieces were set up, ready for battle.

145

They were unlike any I had ever seen. The kings, queens and their courts were all hand-carved, in forms dredged from a clearly remarkable imagination. They were delicately painted and sealed in hard varnish, but there was no doubt as to which side was which.

The black pawns were twisted, leering goblins; the castles were tall forbidding tower; the knights were dragon heads; the bishops were horned, hunched things; the royal pieces were cloaked, and oozed menace from under their twisted crowns. The whites, on the other hand were smooth wee beauties. The pawns were beautifully armoured; the castles were straight and topped with tiny, carved, hand-coloured banners; the knights were plumed; the bishops carried crooks, and had long beards; the Queen was a perfect, narrow-waisted lady, with a wimple, rather than a crown; the white King had long, flowing hair, wore a simple, gold-painted circlet and leaned on a great broadsword.

I picked up the menacing black King. It was surprisingly heavy, and I realised that there was a weight set in its base. I held it up, and gasped at the way its pinprick eyes seemed to follow me, glowering.

'Did you make these?' I asked. 'They're brilliant.'

He smiled, and I could see that he was the sort of bloke who's embarrassed by his talent. 'Thank you. They're just a one-off, though. I couldn't do them commercially. Take too much time. My model soldiers are easier.

'Right, Oz, you're black.' The game didn't last long. He marched his soldiers out methodically, as I pursued my usual tactic of going for a quick kill, crashing my main attacking pieces all around the board, looking for an opening. He took my offensive apart, pawn by pawn, knight after knight, until all but nine of the men were on his side of the board. Finally he zapped me with a Queen–rook move that I saw only when I was beyond redemption.

He nodded as I tipped over my King. 'Excellent. You'll do for my daughter all right. People approach chess in the same way they approach their lives. You, Oz, play with your heart, rather than your head. Exactly like Primavera; you couldn't be better matched.'

Right on cue, my beloved appeared in the doorway. 'Come on you two. Lunch.' She led us through to a long dining room at the rear of the house, where a long table – more Corleone Family than Addams this time – was set for five.

'It's as if we were expected,' I said to Prim; quietly, I thought, but her mother can hear a mouse break wind at the foot of the garden.

'Sunday, Oz,' she boomed. 'We always cook a big bird on Sunday. It does us for a couple of days.' The big bird turned out to have been a goose, but before we got that far we were faced with the sort of thick soup that my Granny Blackstone used to make. You know the kind; you can draw your initials in the middle and they won't go away till you spoon them up. As I tackled and conquered the strong-flavoured goose, I looked out of the window. The Phillips' back garden was of the market variety. On one side vegetables were set out in rows; potatoes, carrots, leeks, pea stalks, runner beans. On the other, there were lines of raspberry canes, with strawberry patches next to the house and rhubarb under the boundary wall.

'What do you do with all that?' I asked Dad Phillips. 'You can't handle it all, surely?'

'Of course we can,' he said. 'We're not completely Norman Rockwell, you know. We do have a freezer. Everything we can't eat fresh goes in there, potatoes included, either cut into chips or sautéed.'

147

Naturally, there were raspberries for desert.

As we sat over our coffee, Mr Phillips looked across the table at Dawn over the top of his big glasses. Suddenly he was stern. 'Now, young lady. Perhaps you'll tell us why we had the police at our door yesterday, looking for you.'

Dawn went white for a second, then flushed bright scarlet.

'Didn't they tell you?' said Prim, with a combative edge to her voice.

At once, Dad Phillips abandoned his attempt to be the heavy father. It isn't a role that suits him, anyway. 'No, they didn't. They said something about wanting her to assist with an enquiry in Edinburgh.'

'Yes, that's right. But it's got nothing to do with Dawn really. A man was found dead in a flat in Ebeneezer Street, on my stair. The police want to talk to all the neighbours, to find out if they saw anything. But Dawn was here when it happened, so she can't tell them anything. End of story.'

I could tell that he didn't believe her. But I could tell also whose word is law in the Phillips family, when push comes to shove, and that, whatever was happening, he trusted her to handle it. Dad and Mum don't really want to play in the Nineties, and sometimes the world frightens Dawn just a bit. If Semple House, Auchterarder, was an independent state, Prim would be Foreign Secretary.

'Poor chap,' he said. 'Yet it was a bit much of the police to come chasing Dawn up here, in the circumstances. Could you two talk to them when you go back to Edinburgh?' He glanced at me.

'Sure,' I said. 'That'll probably keep them happy.'

'What did you tell them?' Prim asked.

'They asked me a straight question, so I gave them a straight answer. I said that Dawn had been here, but that she

148

was away for a day or two with a friend in Perth. I said that she'd be back on Sunday, and we'd ask her to contact them as soon as possible. They seemed happy enough with that.'

'When *are* you two going back?' said Mrs Phillips.

'We thought we'd stay overnight,' said Prim, 'if that's all right?'

'All right! Of course it is. Your bed's made up, Primavera. I put sheets on it after you phoned. Thee's fresh linen under the stair for the fourth bedroom.' My heart sank, and I think my face must have gone down with it, for Prim kicked me under the table. I supped my coffee to cover my tracks.

There's not a lot you can do to escape a Scottish Sabbath, but eventually, after the girls had washed the dishes, Dad had massacred my goblin army on the chess-board a few more times, and we'd had totally unnecessary tea, scones and jam, Prim came up with a cover story. 'Mum, I think I'll take Oz to meet Julia.' It was around 6.30 p.m.

'Who's Julia?' I asked.

'My best pal from school. I visit her every time I'm here. She lives at the other end of town. We'll walk. Dawn, you come too.

'Oz, go and get our stuff out of the car, there's a love.'

Mrs Phillips was crossing the hall when I came back inside. When she noticed that I was carrying just one bag, she glanced at me and I'll swear a tiny smile flickered around the corners of her mouth. I guessed that there was something left of the woman who had christened her daughter after the time of her conception. She's a great believer is Prim's Mum. She believes in God, in her family and in all of life's certainties; the return of the seasons, and all that.

Of course, Julia wasn't in. We could have telephoned first, but we didn't. Instead we walked all the length of

Auchterarder's Main Street to find out, then made a detour up to the Gleneagles Hotel, which turned out to have been our real objective after all.

I thought we'd be lucky to be served in denims, but the Phillips sisters are well known there. We sat in the big bar sipping half-pints of Pimms, which Dawn insisted on buying with her movie money. Eventually I asked her how much she was being paid. When she told me I think she heard me grind my teeth. Sometimes it takes me more than six months to make the dough that Dawn was earning for a couple of weeks' work.

'Don't think it's all like that. Once this gig is over, chances are I'll be back in Edinburgh, doing stock plays at the Lyceum and being paid sweeties for it. That's if I've got a job at all.

'I won't complain if that's how it turns out. I like the Lyceum. You feel really close to your audience there, and the regulars feel close to us. Our Chairman came up with a really good idea last year. He started a theatre club for us performers and for our season ticket holders and regulars. We've got our own bar, and we can go in there after rehearsal – anytime really – and mix with the punters, making them feel part of the theatre family. We get some odd sorts turning out.' Her expression darkened all of a sudden. 'That's where I met Willie.' She sat there for almost a minute, in silence. Prim and I said nothing, letting her come through it in her own time. At last a faint smile returned to her lips. 'Willie. A bird with a broken wing all right.

'But he was just one among many. We've got a real cross-section of members. We've got civil servants, lawyers, a couple of hairdressers, housewives, flash young guys out to pull an actress. We've even got a member who's a prostitute. She offered Rawdon a freebie one night! I doubt if he took her up on it though! Oh yes, and we've got one policeman. A real Mr Plod, but he's dead keen. Surprising: you'd never guess it to look at him. McArthur, his name is.'

My eyebrows rose. 'What! A big beefy bloke with a red face?'

'Yes, that's him. He comes to every play, and he's in the bar about every second night.'

'My God,' I said, shaking my head in disbelief. 'McArse the theatregoer. You never know the hidden depths of people.'

It was just after nine-thirty when we finished our third round of Pimms and decided that it was time to call it quits. Night was still a way off as we strolled up the Gleneagles driveway and out towards the road, but the sun had gone and there were patches of darkness under the trees. If Auchterarder is famous for anything other than Gleneagles, it's because it lays claim to the longest Main Street of any Scottish town. All of it lay between us and Semple House as we turned into it and set off three abreast, with me in the middle and Dawn on the outside.

A pint and a half of Pimms seemed to have relaxed Dawn. As we walked she asked us how we had traced her, and laughed as Prim described our encounter with Rawdon Brooks. 'Poor old Rawdon,' she laughed. 'You shouldn't be hard on him. I know he's outrageous, he's a bit of a junkie, and he could seduce the College of Cardinals, but he's really nice. Gay men can be the kindest people, you know. There's no-one better when it comes to sharing your troubles. No offence, Prim, but they're even better than sisters.

'You can tell them anything you like, and they won't hold it against you, or tell a soul. So many people have cried on Rawdon's shoulders, they must be mildewed. He helped me a lot when I was going through agonies with Willie. He did his

151

best to help Willie too, being a friend, and making him ask himself whether he was certain about what he was doing.'

'A real heart of gold,' I said, and she dug me in the ribs with her elbow.

'So tell me, you two. What d'you think I should do, then?' she asked, lisping slightly.

'No doubt about that,' I said. 'First thing tomorrow you should get your shapely arse back up to Connell or wherever the next stop is, and cuddle up to the leading man. "Tell her if she's got a problem, Old Miles'll sort it out." That's what he said. I'll tell you, I reckon he could, too. When you've got as much clout as Miles Grayson, you can sort out most things.

'Yes, Dawn. You head back to the Highlands and cuddle up to Miles.'

She looked up at me, then across at her sister. 'Hey, Prim,' she called. 'Where did you find this guy? I like the way he thinks!'

We were laughing so loud we might have not heard the car, but there was something about the engine tone that broke through to me, something about the way it kept on revving when the driver should have been changing gear. I looked up, just in time to see a black shape, travelling flat-out, swerve and head towards us, at racing speed, climbing on to the pavement.

If there had been a high wall on the other side of us we'd have been dead. All of us. But, thank God, there was only a low stone thing, with a sickly privet hedge behind it. The car was almost on us as I grabbed each sister around the waist and jerked them off their feet – diving, plunging over the wall and through the hedge. In mid-air, I felt something catch the outside of my left foot, twisting it, but somehow we made it, all three of us, to the other side.

Behind us we heard a crunch, the sound of breaking glass

and the scream of metal as the speeding car crashed into the wall. We lay there breathless waiting for it to stop, but it went roaring on, on down the longest Main Street in any Scottish town, and away into the gathering night.

I helped the girls to their feet and looked around. We were in a long garden. It stretched for at least a hundred yards, up to a big detached villa. We waited for lights to come on but none did. Amazingly, no lights came on in the surrounding houses either. Auchterarder's a bit like that. Plenty of Levites, but not too many Samaritans.

Eventually, I took a chance and stuck my head out of the garden, checking to see if the black car had come back, if it was lying out there, waiting for another shot. I felt like a character in a Stephen King novel.

'Who was it?' said Prim behind me. 'Did you see?' It was remarkable that not one of us thought for a second that it might have been a drunk driver.

'No,' I said. 'Och it was probably a drunk driver.' Even through the gloom, I felt the eyes of the Phillips sisters boring into me.

'Did you get the number?' asked Dawn.

'Do us a favour. I was too busy saving your life.' I shuddered and tried to replay the scene in my mind's eye. Again, I saw the car screaming towards us. I tried to freeze the picture. Suddenly, unexpectedly fragments of detail came back. 'A Mondeo, I think. Navy or black. "N" registered.' I tried to push everything else from my mind. 'The last two registration letters could have been "BL". But I couldn't swear to it.'

' "BL"?' said Dawn. 'Then it could have been hired.'

'How do you work that out?' asked Prim.

'The film unit have hired minibuses. And Miles has a big

153

stretched Ford thing. They all have "BL" registrations. But what does that tell us?'

'It could tell us that whoever did that didn't want to be putting their own car in for repair. Or it could tell us that it was a visiting Yank, driving, pissed, away from Gleneagles.'

We stood there for another five minutes, waiting, listening, watching every passing car, before we braved the road again. My jarred foot pained me with every step I took. We had been walking, or in my case limping, for less than a minute, when a taxi drove by, I hailed it and it stopped. The driver was a guy in his late twenties. He knew Prim and Dawn from school.

As we drove towards Semple House, I squeezed Dawn's hand. 'Hey. Remember what I was saying about cuddling up to Miles.' She nodded. 'I don't think you should wait till morning. I think you should go tonight.'

'Why? You don't think that was meant for me, do you?'

'No, of course not. I can't think why it should be meant for any of us. But whoever that was, it wasn't an autograph hunter. The best place for you is back with the crew.

'Tell your Mum and Dad you have to be back early. Then get on your way. Tonight.'

In which Mother offers black pudding, and we take a decision.

I don't know how long she'd been knocking. The sound started as part of a dream, a nice dream of domesticity, in which Prim and I were, I think, in the process of living happily ever after. I tried to dismiss it, but it was persistent, forcing its way from the back of my mind right up to the front.

Eventually it carried me back to the world of the wide-awake. I propped myself up on an elbow, taking care not to disturb the dozing blonde bundle lying beside me, on top of the quilt. One of Africa's gifts to Primavera is the ability, when she feels secure, to sleep through virtually anything.

'Morning,' I called drowsily to the door.

'Wakey, wakey Oz.' Mum Phillips sounded bright and breezy. 'Breakfast in twenty minutes. D'you like black pudding?' I squeezed my eyes tight to clear them, and looked at my watch on the bedside table. It was ten past eight.

'Thanks,' I called. 'See you there. And, yes, I love black pudding!'

'Good.' There was a pause. 'By the way, you haven't seen my daughter, have you?'

'I'll look under the bed.'

Beside me, Prim was beginning to stir, uncoiling, like a cat, sighing, murmuring, stretching. Eventually she shook her head and looked up at me, puzzled at first, then remembering. She pulled herself up and leaned against the heavy walnut headboard, flinching slightly from the coolness of the wood on her back, even through her nightshirt.

'What are you doing here?' I asked her. 'Have I got that job?'

She smiled, rubbing her eyes. 'I don't think that this is quite the place for the audition!

'Sorry to disappoint you, but I couldn't sleep for thinking about what happened last night. So I came in here, thinking you'd be in the same state. You were out like a light.'

'No imagination,' I said. 'That's my trouble.'

Her right breast hung a few inches away from me. Automatically, as if I had done it a hundred times before, I rubbed my forehead against it, and flicked my tongue across the protuberance of her nipple, through the cotton of her shirt. She shivered, then slid, supply, down the covers once again to lie beside me. I could feel her warm breath on my face as we kissed. Her nightdress, which was no more than a long tee-shirt, had ridden up around her waist. I laid my hand on her naked hip and pulled her closer to me as I kissed her again. Her tongue sought out mine, and her fingers wound through my hair. Suddenly she rolled over on top of me, moving her body against me. I could feel the heat of her through the covers, and her eyes burned into mine.

I smiled, 'What's it to be?' I said. 'Me, or your Mum's black pudding?'

She laughed. 'You lose,' she said, biting the end of my nose, gently. 'For now.' She pushed herself back and sat upright, straddling me. I gasped, and her eyes widened, as her weight bore down on my most critical region. 'It's nice to know I can command your attention when I want to,' she murmured.

'Darling,' I said, 'right now you're commanding a hell of a lot more than my attention!'

Gymnastically, she raised herself up again and swung her legs around to sit on the edge of the bed. When she turned and looked at me again, the tease was gone from her eyes.

'Who, Oz?' she pondered. I had fallen asleep asking myself the same question.

'I don't know,' I said.

'Unless . . .' she said.

'What?'

'No, forget it.'

'Come on!' I grunted. I hate it when someone sets me up and then says, 'No, forget it.'

'Well, *why* would anybody want to kill *us*?'

'What d'you mean?'

'Well, why *would* anyone? Not because of what we know. The only person who knows that *we* know about the money is Ray Archer, and right now we're his only chance of getting it back. And not because of what we've got. This gets complicated, but whoever is after the fiver doesn't necessarily know that *we* know what it's for. And they wouldn't want to kill us, would they, at least until they'd got it?'

'So?'

'So could the driver have been after Dawn?'

'Aw, come on. Who'd want to kill Dawn?' as I said it a thought nagged at my brain.

I looked sideways at Prim and shuddered. 'Ugh! Stop.

You're doing my head in. The main thing is we're all alive, and Dawn's safely off to her movie. Now, if you're still turning down the best offer you've had all day, concentrate on breakfast, and on getting your brain into gear. We've got some decisions to make.'

The tease was back in her eyes. I pushed myself upright and drew her backwards, pulling her down until her head rested on the pillow. Her nightshirt was drawn up higher this time, and the lower swell of her breasts was in view. She looked up at me: all at once, her right hand was under the covers, feeling, seeking, finding. The smile faded to be replaced by something else. I bent over her and kissed her navel, then flicked my tongue into its cavity, then out, then in then out, then . . .

'Ahhh!' she gasped, holding my head with her free hand, rotating her hips beneath me. I slid the nightshirt up, feeling her lift her arms and raise her head and shoulders to assist me. 'Oz!' She hissed, with an edge of hesitancy in her voice, but with overpowering urgency, and without a shred of teasing. The nightshirt stretched taut as it cleared her shoulder, but in a moment her arm was free. I eased myself upright and began to pull back the barrier of linen and blankets which kept us apart. All the while she held on to me, stroking, kneading, until I thought I would burst.

The knock on the door was as vigorous as before. 'Oz! Five minutes.'

'Bugger!' said Primavera and I, in unison.

Prim shook her head in despair. 'Make it fifteen,' she called out to the door. 'Oz has to shave.' She let me go, then sat up and thrust her arm back into her nightshirt.

'Told you this was no place for an audition,' she said, smiling. 'We found out one thing, though.'

'What's that?' I asked. I felt myself subside, experiencing

also the onset of a condition known and dreaded by all men in such a situation.

'You can command my attention as well!'

Semple House has basins in every bedroom. As soon as I felt confident that my boxers had resumed a normal shape, I vaulted out of bed and turned on the hot tap. The water reached near-boiling point, almost instantly.

She sat on the bed, watching me as I lathered my chin. 'Before we got distracted, you were talking about decisions,' she said. 'What sort d'you mean?'

'The sort we've been avoiding until now. Like, where are we going next? Should we tell Archer we've got the fiver? Should we tell the police everything?'

I drew my razor down my cheek, cutting a clean, shiny swathe through the foam.

'What d'you think?'

I could see her in the mirror, holding her chin as she pondered over my questions. 'I don't know. I do know what common sense says. Until now, we've put everything to one side to find Dawn. Now we've done that, and we know that she's safe, and didn't have anything to do with Willie Kane's murder, then as good honest citizens we should say "Sod the reward, sod Archer and his sordid cover-up", and tell the whole story to Mike Dylan.

'And yet . . .' Her reflection swung her legs off the bed and stood up, stretching her arms high above her head, clasping her hands together and pulling them backwards, thrusting out her breasts and tensing the muscles of her groin. 'I don't know, I've got a bad feeling about something.' As I scraped the last of the lather from my top lip, I saw her cross the room. She stood behind me and wrapped her arms around my waist. 'What d'*you* think?'

I disengaged her and turned round, holding her at arm's length. 'I think we should be very careful. We've found Dawn, she's all right, she's got an alibi, and that's good. But it doesn't take away the memory of wee Kane dead in your bed, and it doesn't tell us who killed him. And it doesn't take away what happened last night.

'I've got a bad feeling too. It comes from Dylan suddenly wanting to know about the fiver, and about the fact that he was so keen to find it that he actually broke into my place to search for it.'

She looked up at me. 'So, should we give it to *him*?'

I shook my head. 'No, that's the last thing we should do. Dylan didn't have a clue about it on Thursday morning, yet on Friday he's turning over Edinburgh, trying to find it. So who told him what it was worth? It's a cert. that Kane was killed for that note, only whoever did it couldn't find it. We only have it now because clumsy Mr Plod knocked over your muesli jar. So who knew about it? One, I did; two, Raymond Archer did.

'So is there a link between him and Dylan, or someone else? God knows, but I think we should try to find out too.'

'You don't think Archer could have killed Kane himself?'

'Nah. I really don't see that. Why should he involve me if he was going to kill the wee fella?'

She looked at me doubtfully. 'In that case, who?'

'Let's wait and see. Dawn said something yesterday that could give us a clue.'

'What was that?'

'All in good time, my dear.'

'Oz, don't be mysterious!' She stepped close against me once more and kissed my chest. Down in the jungle, a natural force began to stir once more. With a huge effort of will, I steered her towards the door.

'Go, woman,' I declaimed, 'and stop trying to seduce me. After breakfast, we'll work out a game plan. Meantime, I can smell that black pudding.'

Dad and Mum Phillips are creatures of habit. Their days seem to be more organised than anyone's I've ever met. Breakfast is one of their rituals, and that morning, they clearly enjoyed sharing it with their older child, and with the big, tousle-headed cuckoo who sat beside her at the dining table.

The black pudding tasted as good as it smelled. Mrs Phillips dished it up together with scrambled eggs and mushrooms, and thick slices of toast. We made small talk as we ate. Dad asked me some more about my work, my family, where I lived, gently filling in the gaps in his knowledge. He looked impressed when I said my father was a dentist.

Mum muttered that it was a pity that Dawn had rushed off. 'That's her all over. Impetuous. One minute she's going back on Monday morning, next she has to be there for early-morning run-through.'

At five to nine, it was suddenly all over. 'Right,' said Mum, standing up abruptly. 'Dad and I are off to work. The washing up's all yours. Come, David. We'll be in the studio; let us know when you're ready for the road.'

I washed, I dried, and Prim supervised, eventually condescending to stack the plates in the kitchen cupboard. 'Right,' she said, when she was finished. 'Decision time. What do we do now, Oz?'

I reached out a hand for her. You may have noticed that I'm very tactile, as far as Prim is concerned at least. I'm never happier than when I'm touching her.

'I've been thinking about that,' I said. 'I reckon it's time for me to treat Ray Archer to another performance of my Daft

161

Laddie act. There are some things we need to know, and I reckon he might be able to help us . . . as long as he doesn't know he's doing it!'

In which Ray Archer is immersed in his own Genius.

We said our farewells to Mum and Dad Phillips, in the spacious attic studio which they shared. His bench and lathe was on one side, her Apple Mac computer on the other.

'You'll take care of the police business for Dawn, will you, Primavera?' Mr Phillips asked, still a touch anxiously.

'No, Dad,' she said. 'Dawn's going to phone them this morning. We agreed that was the best way to handle it.'

'And you, Primavera,' said her mother. 'What will you do when you get back to Edinburgh? Start looking for a hospital job?'

'Give me a break, Mum. I think I've earned a holiday over the last year.'

'Yes, I suppose you have. Don't let it last too long, though. You know what they say about the Devil and idle hands.'

Prim laughed, and dug me in the ribs with an elbow. 'Hear that, Devil?' she murmured.

Rather than retrace our route to Perth, we took the twisty road down from Auchterarder through the hills, and picked up the motorway just south of Kinross. I tried to call Archer on the mobile, but the cloud was low, and we were in a dead zone for transmission until we were in sight of the Forth Bridge.

Eventually, I got through. When he came on the line, he spoke quietly, as if he had company. 'I need to see you,' I said. 'I've found Kane's girlfriend. She was out of town when he was killed, and she doesn't have the fiver. I have to meet you today, to talk about what we do next.'

'Okay,' Archer whispered. 'But not in the office. Meet me at midday, in the Abbotsford.'

I hate going into pubs at lunchtime. Nearly always, I feel guilty, and wonder about everyone else who's in there taking in alcohol in the middle of what should be a working day. (Oz Blackstone, closet prude!) The Abbotsford's an exception though. It's a real characterful place, still in its original wood panelling, with a big oval bar, and a few booths with benches for those who prefer to drink sitting down.

Prim and I agreed that there were no plus points to be gained from introducing her to Archer at that stage, so when we reached Rose Street, she ducked into Marks & Spencer to replenish her knicker stock while I shouldered my way through the brass-handled double doors of the old pub.

The Abbotsford was still relatively quiet; the place smelled of mutton pies heating in the oven and beans on the hob, being made ready to be hoovered up by the lunchtime rush. There was no sign of Archer in the bar, but when I looked into the back room, I found him there, sat, alone, at a table, nursing a half-pint of Guinness.

He offered me a drink, but I said a quick 'No thanks' and sat down facing him. As usual there were no preliminaries. 'Where did you find the girl?' he asked at once.

I treated myself to the luxury of telling him the truth. 'She

164

was up in Perthshire, with her parents. She was there at the time Kane was killed, and she can prove it.'

He looked at me over his Guinness. 'D'you think she was in the know about it, though?'

'No chance. She wanted shot of the wee man all right, but not that way.'

'She said she doesn't have the fiver?'

'That's right.'

'And you believed her?' There was more than an edge of doubt in his tone.

'Yes. Kane spun her a story about wanting to squirrel his money away from his wife, before he left her. He told her she'd have every penny, otherwise. Dawn's an actress. She's got an active imagination, so it wasn't difficult for her to take his story at face value. She was sorry for him so she agreed to help him set up the account. When she got back, she gave him the fiver, and that's the last she saw of it.'

'Are you trying to tell me she doesn't know about the missing money?'

'That's what she said, and from the way she looked at me when I asked her about it, I believe her.'

His look was one of pure scorn. I was annoyed even before he opened his mouth. Afterwards, I was downright angry. 'Come on Blackstone!' He spat it out, his eyes narrowing. 'Who are you trying to kid? Know what, I reckon you're shagging this tart now. I reckon you and she have done a deal about the money!'

Temper and Oz are not normally associated, one with the other. I've never taken a pop at anyone in my life, but I've never come closer to it than I did with Ray Archer right then. Instead, and it was as if my hand made its own decision, independent of my brain, I picked up his Guinness and threw it in his face.

He started off his bench. I thought he was going to take a swing at me, and so, before he was even halfway upright, I shoved him back on to his pin-striped arse.

Now it was me spitting out the words. I don't know whose voice I was using, but it didn't sound like mine. 'You say that just once more, pal, and I'm going to make a phone call to a guy I know on *Scotland on Sunday*. Then I'm going to see my lawyer. After that, he and I are going to see Inspector Dylan.

'If you want to end up twisting in the wind, with all your partners beside you, then just keep it up.'

His head went down; he took his hankie from his breast pocket and mopped his dripping face. 'I'm sorry, Oz,' he said softly, gazing at the table, not at me. In those seconds his tone changed from aggressive to wheedling. I disliked that just as much. 'I shouldn't have said that. My firm has ten partners and forty employees. The career of every one of them is riding on my shoulders, and it's getting to me. You're the last person I should be upsetting. Please forgive me.'

His protestations of concern for his workforce were lost on me. He was only thinking about money . . . his money. 'Level with me, Mr Archer,' I said, recovering the normal Oz tone, 'how long do I have to get your funds back?'

'A week at the outside. Our client's abroad just now. He'll be back in Edinburgh in ten days.'

'And if we don't get it back, what's the down-side? Do you really go bust?'

He shrugged his shoulders. 'If you can't get that money back by next Monday, my partners and I, and that means mostly me, will have to cover the loss and probably pay a premium to buy back the stock that Kane sold. With luck, we'll keep the firm afloat, but . . .' He gazed up at me, with what he hoped would look like desperation.

166

'At the moment, only you, my financial controller and I know about this thing. If I have to tell my partners, that makes it all the more dangerous for us. After that, just one tongue loosened in the Drum and Monkey by one pint too many and it could be all up for Black and Muirton.'

A sudden thought ran down my spine, like a mouse with very cold feet.

'Tell me about your financial controller.'

Archer smiled, wanly. 'Jerry? No, Oz. Forget it. Jerry Hannah's sixty-nine years old, and he has a bad heart. Apart from all that, he's the tightest-mouthed old bastard I know. If you told Jerry a secret he wouldn't even repeat it back to you.'

'And you've told no-one else?'

He shook his head, but there was a hesitation there. 'No. Only my wife. I told her the whole story last Monday, as soon as I'd pieced it all together, about the theft, about Berners and the bank account, and how Kane and the girl had set it up. I told her I was going to hire you to get the money back.' He gave me one of those man to man glances. 'I had to confide in someone. Anyway, Marian and I make a point of having no secrets.'

I gave him the nod he expected.

'I don't suppose Willie Kane would have told anyone about his scam. I mean he and Mrs Kane weren't exactly on pillow-talk terms any more, were they?'

He gave a short, choked off laugh. 'No indeed. God, when I think about it, poor Marian. Getting my worries and Linda's at the same time. I told you, she's Linda Kane's best friend. We're near neighbours, so they see each other every day. Linda used to work for Black and Muirton, you know. That's how she and Willie met. She was his secretary. The odd couple, and no mistake.'

'Mrs Kane must have been pretty upset when he walked out on her. Then with him being killed, your wife must have had a hard time with her.'

Archer snorted. 'From what Marian says, "grief-stricken" isn't quite the term for her. She was absolutely furious when he left. But "incandescent", was how Marian described her after the murder. I suppose we all build walls against bereavement in different ways.'

Suddenly he snapped back into his businesslike mode. 'So what are you going to do next, Oz? The trail of that banknote must be pretty cold, if Willie's girl doesn't have it.'

So far, I had gone through our conversation without telling Archer a single porky-pie; now I was struggling to keep up my run. I could have said, 'Look Ray, it's all right, I've got the fiver,' but something held me back. Probably it was the fact that somewhere in the city, outside the Abbotsford, was the guy who had killed Kane to get that banknote. That and the thought that, one way or another, unwittingly or wittingly, Archer must have put him on the trail. I thought about Kane, and that knife, and all of a sudden my tongue stuck to the roof of my mouth. The less Archer knew, the safer it would be for Prim and me.

I gazed at him with an expression that was meant to be contemplative, but which really hid the fact that I hadn't a clue what to do next. But at last, it came to me. 'I think it's time I paid a call on a lady,' I said, in Private Eye-speak, turned on my heel and walked out of the pub, leaving him to the impossible task of wiping drying Guinness stains off a pale blue shirt.

In which we meet the Widow Kane
and find her wanting
in the grief department.

'**O**z, I know you're daft; you don't have to go proving it all the time.' From the moment of our meeting, Prim's faith in my judgement has been touching. 'What will we say to the woman?'

'I don't know for sure. I just think we should go along to offer our sympathies. Remember what Dawn said about her. She was two-timing Willie, according to him at least.'

Primavera looks wonderful when her smile is just about to erupt into laughter. When she throws her head back and laughs it sounds like the pealing of a chime of bells. Right at that moment, the ringers had a good grip on the ropes.

'So we just walk in there, and ask her about it, do we?'

'Not quite, but there's one thing we might learn, if we play our cards right. Just think back to what Dawn said about her.' She thought for only a few seconds, then caught on. Much quicker than her sister, is Prim. When it comes to it, she's much quicker than me. 'I remember now. And you think . . .'

When you're really in love, telepathy is a perfectly feasible proposition.

We found the address with no difficulty at all. In the back of the car, we still had a copy of the *Evening News* which carried the report of his identification, complete with a photo of *Chez* Kane. Even for a stockbroker, it looked quite a place. It was a big villa along Ravelston Dykes, one of those streets in Edinburgh where the poor folk aren't encouraged to get out of their cars.

As I parked the Nissan, defiantly, Prim gazed at the house through the wrought-iron railings which topped the small garden wall. She whistled softly. 'Poor Willie must really have been stuck on our Dawn to walk out of this pile,' she whispered.

'Or he must really have hated his wife,' I said.

The only downmarket thing about the house was the car in the driveway. It was a silver Calibra, where you'd have expected a Five-series Beamer at the very least. But, still, it was top-of-the-range, with a personalised 'LBK' number plate.

I took a quick peek through the living-room window as we approached the front door, hustling along in the light rain, which had been threatening all day. Where Semple House was genuine Charles Addams, 'Achnasheen', for thus it had been named by a fanciful builder, was genuine *Vogue*. The furniture was modern but nondescript, white leather settees, a dull highboard, a hi-fi rack and speakers against the far wall. Prim tugged me towards the front door and rang the bell.

It took a second ring before the door was opened, by a reddish-haired woman. She leaned against the jamb, perspiring and breathing heavily. She looked well on the fleshy side in her leotard and tights, ankle-warmers and trainers, her bosom jiggling formidably as it rose and fell. In the background, an aerobics tape pounded on loudly.

She looked at us as she recovered her wind. For the faintest moment I thought I saw alarm in her eyes; but probably I imagined it. This was a woman who would not be alarmed by heavy machine gun fire. 'Yes?' she gasped, eventually.

'Mrs Kane?' I asked. She nodded, and I ploughed on as wide-eyed and friendly as could be. 'Sorry if it's an inconvenient time, but we wondered if we might have a word with you?'

She was breathing normally now, and looked formidably hostile. 'You're not more bloody press, are you?' I noticed that her voice was harder than the norm among Ravelston matrons.

'Heavens no,' I said airily.

'Oh Christ, not the fucking Witnesses, surely! Sunday was yesterday, chum.'

I smiled, trying to appease her. 'No, Mrs Kane, we're not witnesses. Not that sort, anyway. We, I, wanted to talk to you about your husband. My name's Oz Blackstone. I don't know if the police told you, but it was us who found Mr Kane.'

The hostility lessened a bit, but she was still a long way from offering an embrace. 'I see. So? Do you expect a fucking reward?'

I took a deep breath. 'Well, my girlfriend and I thought we should maybe come along to see you, just to, well comfort you if we could.'

'Do I look as if I need comforting?'

I almost told her she looked as if she needed a couple of weeks on Slimfast, and a compassion transplant, but I held back. We hadn't come just to be slung off her doorstep. Eventually she gave in. 'Oh, come on in, if you must. The Cindy Crawford workout's left me shagged out anyway.' She turned in the doorway and pressed a TV remote. In the background, Cindy was cut off in her splendid prime.

She led us into the 'no imagination' living room. A packet of Benson and Hedges lay on the mantelpiece. She took out a fag and lit it with a big Ronson table model, offering the pack to us as she inhaled.

'So,' she said, as the blue smoke gave the room its only real colour. 'What did you want to tell me about the dear departed?'

'Well, we thought you might like to know that it seemed as if he didn't suffer, that it was pretty quick.'

She took another drag, and looked at me as if I was an idiot. Right then, that was how I felt; if you called Linda Kane a hard cow, you'd be insulting bovines everywhere. 'I'd worked that one out, son. Who d'you think identified the little shit? I imagine that if someone skewers your top-piece you go straight to the Pearly Gates, no stopping.

'More's the pity,' she added with venom.

'Oh, come on Mrs Kane,' surprising myself by coming to the adulterous embezzler's defence.

'Come on nothing. The little bastard left me. He walked out on me for some fucking tart . . . on me! After all I've done for him. I *made* him at Black and Muirton, you know. The number of times I covered up for him. To look at him you'd never have thought he'd the brains to . . .' She stumbled, very slightly, then caught herself, '. . . put his hat on the right way round.

'Nearly said something rude there.' She added, with a coyness that sat on her as easily as a nun on a rodeo bull.

'So you found him, did you?' She looked at Prim. 'That means you, dear, must be that little tart's sister. Little bastard or not he was *my* little bastard; And anyone who takes what's mine . . . Fucking little tart!'

I held my breath and waited for Prim to drive the woman's nose up into her brain. But Linda Kane saved the situation, and herself. 'Look, I'm sorry to be so blunt, talking about her like that, but woman to woman, you must know how I feel. And I know you can't pick your relatives.'

Somehow, Prim managed to look at the floor and say nothing. Then she turned away, and walked a few paces across the room, to the tasteless high-board. There were several silver-framed photographs on a shelf in the middle. She picked one up, and looked at it, then held it up so that Linda Kane and I could both see it. It showed a girl, a mature schoolgirl, in a blazer shirt and tie. 'Is this your daughter?'

Linda smiled. 'Do I look old enough? Yes, well I suppose I am. No, dear, that's me, when I was head girl at Mary Erskine. Let's see. That'll have been taken in 1975.'

I whistled. 'You've worn well then.'

She looked at me with the nearest thing I've seen to a leer on a woman. 'Flattery, son, will get you most places. But not here; not here. I like my men a bit older than you, and a bit bulkier too.'

She took the photo from Prim. 'Now, if that's all you've got to tell me, thank you for coming, but I'm due for a cut at Charlie Kivlin's in an hour.' She ushered us smoothly back to the door.

'Must look my best for the funeral, after all. It's at Mortonhall, on Friday. I've got a fair idea what I'm going to do with the ashes afterwards.' She made an unmistakable flushing movement with her right hand.

'Cheerio, then. If you want to come to the funeral you'll be welcome. The senior partner's talking about having a reception afterwards in the office. That's a bloody sight more than *I'd* do for him.'

She closed the door on us with something grotesque, that we took for a smile.

We hustled down the path to the garden gate as fast as we could and dived into the Nissan, which sat self-consciously under the trees. As soon as we were inside, I looked across at Prim, straight-faced. 'Widow of the Year, eh?' That was enough; we erupted in hoots of laughter.

'God,' she gasped at last, still convulsing, 'I actually feel happy for Willie Kane. Imagine, if Dawn had chucked him out before she left and he'd been forced to go back to that! Whoever killed him did him a favour.'

'Aye, but he did one for her too. With him dead, she'll have the house, free and clear.'

'And what more could she be after?' muttered Prim, ominously.

'Ah, hold on though,' I said, trying to keep her enthusiasm in check. 'She said nothing at all to show that she knows about the theft, or the fiver. She connected you to me, remember, and that's the story the police will have told her, about you and I finding him when we got back from the airport.'

'So what? No, Oz. I'd put nothing past that woman. If Mrs Archer told her about the theft, the bank account and everything, she could have been signing Kane's death warrant. Wish we knew a bit more about the boyfriend though. That's another thing we didn't find out.'

I looked at her, happy in the knowledge that I was about to score a point. 'Remember what Dawn said about him, though. Head boy and head girl at the same time.'

'Yes, I remember; but you remember, Mr Clever Dick. Mary Erskine's an all-girl school. My dumb sister must have got it wrong.'

'Ah Miss Clever . . . eh, Clever whatever. Mary Erskine's

run by the Merchant Company, and there's a partner boys' school less than a mile away. Stewart's-Melville; it's right at the end of this road, in fact. So . . .'

She was like a kid on a treasure hunt. 'So why don't we just head along there now and see what we can find out?'

In which the Old School Archives gives us an answer we don't fancy . . . not one bit.

Daniel Stewart's and Melville College, to give it its full, lengthy title, was formed by the amalgamation of two smaller Merchant Company schools, when economies of scale began to mean something even in the select world of Edinburgh private education.

It's housed in a fine old building on the Queensferry Road, a rectangle with copper-domed towers on each corner. As we reached it, the mothers of its primary school children were just beginning to gather in their second-hand Volvo estates. For some of them, picking up Junior and chewing the fat with the other Mums was probably the highlight of the day. There were so many of them gathered there that we had to park illicitly in the Tourist Board Headquarters and walk back.

The School Office was a slightly chaotic room. That meant that it was like all the school offices I've ever seen, only the accents were more refined, and the weans were better dressed . . . more uniformly, you might say.

The junior secretary was a friendly girl. 'How can I help

you?' she said, and we both knew that she meant it, relieved to be dealing with people from the outside world.

Prim looked at me. I looked at Prim. In the same instant we realised we'd gone barrelling in there without a cover story. 'No, you go on,' said my partner, dropping me in it. Fortunately, my natural glibness, formed out of years spent trying to chat girls just like this one out of their knickers, came surging to the surface. I gave her my best pre-coital smile, the one that says, '*Would you be interested in what I've got here!*'

'My friend and I are researching for a magazine article,' I said, inspirationally. 'We have a commission from the *Sunday Times* supplement for a piece which takes the attitudes of senior-school pupils from the mid-70s and compares them with today's generation.

'We're asking a few schools if they can put us in touch with their head boys and head girls from those times, so that we can set up interviews. We've just seen the head girl of 1975 at Mary Erskine, and she suggested that we should look up her opposite number here.

'Is there any possibility that you could give us his name?'

The girl smiled at me. I could tell that I'd have been in with a chance there.

She put a hand to her chin, as if she was thinking about it, but I knew the answer already. 'I'm sure that I can lay hands on the School Yearbook for 1975,' she said. 'Wait a minute.' She hurried off.

'Smooth-talking bastard,' Prim muttered under her breath as the girl disappeared.

It was only a minute, too. She came rushing back, pink-cheeked and triumphant. 'I knew we had one left. It is only one, though. I can't let you take it away, but I can photocopy pages if you'd like.'

She handed it across the wooden counter. I took it, and noticed that my hand was shaking, very slightly. I held it out so that Prim could see and flicked through the pages until I found the index. 'Captains Courageous' began on page twenty, after the Rector's report on the year.

Naturally, the Head Boy was the first entry. The outstanding chap of the year, beyond a doubt. Captain of Rugby, Captain of Cricket, Captain of Squash, School Athletics Champion, Leader of the Debating team, an all-rounder of the sort in which schools like Stewart's-Melville rejoice. A veritable hero, in fact.

There was a photograph too. He stood there in blazer, decorated with his many sporting colours, slim, squared-jawed, clear-eyed, a man-boy on the verge of a career of leadership in whatever profession he chose. And below the photograph, in rich italics, a caption.

'Head of School, 1974–75. Richard Ross.'

Prim gasped and looked up at me. 'That's Superintendent . . .'

I closed the book. 'Yes, partner. I was afraid it would be him. That's who's got Mike Dylan shitting himself trying to find that fiver. And that's who's been crumpling the sheets with Linda Kane, just like they did twenty years ago.'

We had our backs to the girl, so she couldn't hear us. 'Our FP club keeps very good records,' she said. 'I'm sure they could help you find him.' Helpful to the end.

I handed her back the yearbook. 'That's all right, dear,' I gave her a '*goodnight*' smile. 'Right now, I'm more worried about this chap finding us.' I could feel her eyes in my back, wrinkling with bewilderment, as Prim and I hurried away.

In which plans are made for flight.

'D'you think Linda'll tell him we've been to see her?'
'Abso-bloody-lutely, my darling.' I checked my watch.
'About half an hour ago, I reckon.'

She looked at me; not scared, but anxious. 'We're in trouble, Oz, aren't we?'

'Right up to our pretty little chins, Primavera. You get the picture, yes?'

I didn't need to spell out anything. 'Oh yes, I get it. Mr Archer pours out all his troubles to Mrs Archer. Mrs Archer tells her outraged friend Linda, all about the theft, the account and the banknote. *And* she tells her that Oz Blackstone, PI, is hot on the trail. Linda tells her boyfriend, Superintendent Ross.

'I imagine that gave them a wonderful idea: that they should beat you to it, get rid of the wee chap for good and pick up his money at the same time. Is that how you see it?'

'Sure is. How do you think they went about it.'

'I'd guess that she phoned Willie, and told him she wanted

to see him, alone. Lucky Linda: Dawn was away, so Willie said, "Okay, come to the flat on Wednesday." You said that when you phoned in the evening a woman answered the phone. That must have been her. Think back,' she said. 'Was it?'

I thought back. 'I couldn't swear to it,' I said, honestly. 'It was a funny voice.'

But Prim was in full flow. 'I guess she must have turned on her fading charms for her husband. Something like, "Please come home, Willikins! Let me show you how sorry I am." From the way it looked, Willie fell for it, and . . .' She grimaced, and faltered. I picked up the story.

'The wee man's crowning glory is in the ascendant, when . . . Linda's left the front door on the latch. Ricky Ross slips into the house, and into the bedroom. Poor wee Willie has the orgasm of his life . . . probably Linda does too, for that matter.'

Prim looked up at me. The windows of the Nissan were misting up. I was glad that no-one could see in, otherwise they'd have thought we were having a serious argument. 'There's no other explanation is there?'

'No. None at all. After they killed him, they'd have searched for the fiver. I bet they looked everywhere but in that muesli jar. I suppose Ross asked Dylan next day to report on every single thing his people had found, and Dylan must have mentioned the torn banknote. Hence his sudden interest in getting it back.

'High-flying DIs can be brought down fast if they upset the wrong superintendent. I imagine they can be scared right out of their Loake moccasins too, if they upset Ricky Ross.'

'Can we prove any of this?'

'Not a cat's chance in hell, my dear. We're the ones holding the hot fiver, remember.'

I must have sounded more than a bit frantic, because she took my hand, and wound her fingers through mine, rubbing, soothing. 'So what do we do now, Maestro?'

'We get the hell out of town, chum, that's what we do. Just two calls, and then we're away. Off to do the only thing we can; off to Switzerland to get that money. Agreed?'

She seemed to think about it, for about two seconds. 'Agreed. I guess it's gone too far for us just to give Archer back the fiver.'

'Yes. Ross would probably arrest all of us for being parties to a theft, just for spite. Alternatively he might just kill us. We've got to get the money out of his reach. That's the only answer.'

She nodded. 'Okay. You said we're going to make two calls before we go? Where?'

'I'm going to phone Ali and get him to pick up our passports from the loft. Then we're off to see a laundry lady I know. It's one thing being fugitives, but it's something else wearing last weekend's clothes!'

In which Jan's open secret is revealed to Prim, and in which we find that the heavy has picked up our trail.

After the break-in there was no way we were going back to the loft. We reckoned that there was too big a risk of Ross having it watched.

Rather than use my mobile – that's how paranoid I was – I phoned Ali from a public call-box near Haymarket.

'What's going on, Oz?' My pal was concerned. 'What sort of bother are you and the bird in?'

'Nae bother, Ali, nae bother at all. The flat's such a mess just now that we couldn't face it. We're heading off for a holiday. You'll keep on looking after the green one for us, will you?'

'Aye, of course I will. Ah don't believe a fuckin' word you're telling me, but then you always were a hare-brained bugger, Blackstone. Ah like this "us" stuff, though. It's about time you had somebody holdin' your joystick, permanent-like. She's the real thing, this lassie, is she?'

'She sure is, pal. I'm glad you approve. It's been worrying me all weekend.'

'Sarky bastard! Here, she hasna' got a sister has she?' If only you knew, my dusky China.

'Was he there?' Prim asked as I got back into the Nissan.

'Ali's like the Windmill, love; never closed. He's a good lad, for a grocer. I'd have asked him to bring us some fresh clothes, but if anyone is watching the loft it'd give the game away.'

She nodded, surprised by my unaccustomed thoroughness. There's nothing like a good dose of fear for sharpening the mind . . . and loosening the bowels. 'Where does Jan live?' she asked, as I pulled away from the kerb. 'I take it Jan is your laundry lady.'

'Who else? Her place is in Castle Terrace.'

'It isn't five o'clock yet. Will she be home?'

'With a bit of luck. Jan's a jobbing accountant. She does my tax work as well as my books. Apart from me, she's got a nice wee client list. She does quite a bit of her work at home, so she might well be there. If she isn't we'll go for a walk in Princes Street Gardens.'

She laid a hand, gently on my thigh, as I drove. 'Oz, how will Jan be about me? She was nice enough when we met, but turning up on her doorstep with one bag between us and our dirty laundry, that's something different. I mean you and she have done some heavy breathing together in the past. Are you sure she doesn't still hope you might wind up together. I know her Mum does . . . or did, anyway.'

I smiled at her. 'Don't worry about it. Jan and I are a sister and brother act; okay, we've been incestuous now and again, but that's in the past. Anyway, her heart belongs to another.'

Her eyebrows arched, perfectly. 'What d'you mean?'

'You'll find out.'

There was an empty bay across the street from Jan's place. I put a parking ticket in my windscreen and kept my fingers crossed that my tax disc would attract no fresh attention. Just as I was about to lock up a heavy shower of rain came out of nowhere. I grabbed my anorak and Prim's jacket from the back seat and hustled us both across the street.

Jan's flat is on the second floor. The label beside the entryphone button read 'Turkel/More'. Prim looked at it in surprise as I pushed the plastic stud. 'You mean she lives with someone?'

'That's right. She has done for the last four years. It's a bit turbulent from time to time, but overall they're pretty happy.'

Jan's voice sounded like everyone else's on the wrong end of an entryphone: a bit like a polite Dalek. 'Yes?'

'Hi Jan, it's me and one other. Can we come up?'

There was no answer, only the buzz of the release button being pressed, and a click as the door catch sprung. Jan's stairway is a lot nicer than mine. It's carpeted and there's a chair and cut flowers on each landing. She was waiting for us in the doorway as we reached the second floor, dressed in a white blouse and tight fawn skirt, which showed off her long legs. Jan's legs are her best point, and the rest of her is pretty near to competition class too. 'Hi pal. Hi Prim.' She nodded towards the bag. 'Planning a long stay?'

I was going to spin her a yarn about my Bendix being knackered, but the truth slipped out when I wasn't looking. 'We need some help. Can we run this lot through your washing machine?'

'Sure,' she said, ushering us into the narrow hall. I led the way straight through to the kitchen. 'What's the problem? Mum said you two showed up out of the blue on Friday night.

'Here, that reminds me. What's the score with your Dad and my Mother? I'm beginning to wonder about them.'

'Work it out, Janet. Pre-crumblies can get up to the

naughtiness too. When's she going to make an honest man of him? That's what I want to know.'

She threw her hands up to her face in a comic gesture and dropped into broad Fife. 'My Goad! Can you imagine fit they'll say in Enster, like!'

'You know what they're like. They have to have someone to talk about.' I emptied the bag into the washing machine, loaded Ariel into the sachet thingy, and dialled up a quick wash–dry programme.

Jan gave each of us a beer from the fridge, then pointed us towards the living room, while she went into the bathroom. 'Lock the door this time!' I called after her.

I watched Prim as she looked around Jan's sitting room. You couldn't imagine a bigger contrast to Linda Kane's severe salon. Everything about it fits everything else, and everything in it was chosen for pleasure not appearance. There's a small sofa and two recliner armchairs, all in soft grey fabric, and set around a low coffee table. The floor's varnished but mostly covered by a huge Indian carpet. Over the fireplace, there's an original oil of a beach scene, and a few very tasty watercolours are hung around the walls. The inlaid sideboard was hand-made by a guy in Musselburgh. I'll never forget Jan telling me how much it had cost.

'This is lovely,' said Prim. 'It's saying something to me, but I'm not sure what it is.'

'You'll find out soon enough,' I said. She took hold of my shirt front, and would have had more out of me, if Jan hadn't come in just then.

She looked at us thoughtfully, for a few seconds. 'Yes, Mum was right. About you two, I mean. She phoned me to tell me that Oz had met his match at last. She approves. So, by the way, do I,' she added, in a very matter-of-fact tone. 'Not least because, hopefully, it'll let Mother get me sorted out in her head.' Before Prim could follow up the begged question she changed the subject.

'Right, fugitives. What's the story?'

I know three people in the world who could have handled the truth about our predicament. Happily Jan's one of them. So I pulled Prim on to the sofa beside me and we told her; just like we'd told my Dad, only this time there was an important fact to add which two days earlier had been simply a hunch, plus the part about our narrow escape in Auchterarder.

When we had finished, Jan spread herself in her recliner, her skirt riding away up over her thighs, and looked at us. 'Astounded', just about covered her expression. Her eyes narrowed as she focused on me. 'You know, Oz, I was starting to think that you were turning into a young fogey. A BYF; know what I mean . . . Boring Young Fart. Now here you are, trippin' over corpses, boakin' on traffic wardens, accessory after God knows how many facts, and on the run from a renegade copper.

'Sunshine, you don't just turn over a new leaf. You turn over the whole fuckin' tree!'

She stood up, smoothing down her skirt. 'So what can I do to help?'

'You're doing it. We've decided to head south as fast as we can, with the clothes we've got in that bag. As soon as they're dry, we'll be off.'

'How are you for cash?'

'No problem there. I've got my chargecard, and my PIN number'll work in Europe. Coffee and a sandwich would go down well though.'

She shook her head. 'I can do better than that. I was making a stir fry tonight; I can stretch it to do four. Come on.' She led

189

us back through to the kitchen and busied herself washing and slicing vegetables. Jan's as good a cook as her Mum, but from a different era. Where Auntie Mary works miracles with baking tins and saucepans, Jan tends to use a Wok.

We did our best to help. Prim skinned and boned the monkfish, while I tackled the tough job, cooking the rice. I was watching it intently, and so I didn't see the figure when first she appeared in the doorway.

'Hello Oz. I thought that was your limo outside.'

Anoushka Turkel and I had a difficult relationship until Prim came along. Where Jan's Mum probably saw me as a figure of hope, I'm sure that to Anoushka, I was something of a threat. The old boyfriend, the ever open door when things erupted between them as sometimes they have done, or when Jan's bisexuality caught up with her and she needed a man.

There's nothing bi- about Anoushka. She's a lesbian, and not in the least uncertain, or self-conscious about it. She's a very serious person – a smile from Anoushka's like a rain-storm in the Sahara – but she's kind and she loves Jan to bits. And Jan loves her too. Early on, when first they met, she and I discussed how she felt.

How could I forget! We were in bed together at the time.

As a lover, Jan was one of those people who put everything into it, without ever really getting there herself. I never made the Earth move for her as memorably as she did for me. It was the same that night, only this time I sensed that Jan wasn't putting quite as much into it as usual. So I asked her what was wrong and, being Jan, she told me: how she'd met this corporate lawyer in the office where she was working at the time, and how they'd gone for a few drinks, and how one thing had led to another, and how she'd had the first real, full-blown, screaming orgasm of her life.

I don't think I handled it too well – well, I mean, what bloke would? – until she told me that the corporate lawyer was a woman. Somehow – and I've never figured out how or why – that made it tolerable in a way. With macho rivalries out of the way, I understood what she was saying, and I did my best to help her. I didn't exactly encourage her to set up home with Anoushka, but I said that if she loved her, it was okay with me. When Auntie Mary found out, and it all blew up at home, I stood up for her, and that helped her. Anoushka's never been to Anstruther, but at least after a sticky spell, things are all right between Jan and her Mum.

Of course, the fact that I wasn't in love with Jan helped me be the Boy Scout through it all. Yet I can't deny that on the odd occasion during the year when my doorbell rang late of an evening, and she was there, wearing a look that told me she had a change of knickers and tights in her handbag, well, it didn't half pump up the male ego. Anoushka must have suspected that we had the odd encounter, but, whether out of fear or consideration I don't know, she never raised the subject.

Now she stood there in the kitchen doorway, giving me her odd sizing-up look once again, trying to gauge the significance of Oz Blackstone in her kitchen, helping her girlfriend prepare supper. And then Prim, seeing my gaze, stepped out from behind the door.

A bad analogy, I know, but I took the bull by the horns. I stepped forward and kissed her on her high Slavic cheekbone. 'Hi, Noosh,' I said, as warmly as I could. Then I took my new lady's hand and drew her to me. 'This is Primavera. We're in lurv. Prim, this is Anoushka, Jan's partner.'

Noosh looked at us, stood there together, in total surprise. And then she smiled. It was raining in the Sahara again. 'Well goot for you,' she said, in her funny accent, with its hint of her

Eastern European origins. I reckon that was the most sincere thing she's ever said to me.

'Jan never said about you,' she added, as if to explain her surprise. 'So what brought you to see us. Your good news?'

'That and a knackered washing machine,' said Prim.

'Ah! But you stay to supper?' We both nodded. 'Good. Excuse me, I must change. Back in a minute, Jan darling.' She patted her grey suit, which matched the streaks in her hair, and walked through to their bedroom.

'Oz,' she called through. 'I hope you have that car MOT-d.'

'Yeah. I'm still waiting for my tax disc, but it's okay. Why d'you ask?'

She stepped back into the kitchen, wearing a light dress. ''Cause when I got home there was a policeman in uniform giving it a funny look. I don't think that he was looking at the tax disk, more the number. You don't report it stolen to claim the insurance, no?'

I didn't say a word. Instead I strode back through to the living room and peered out into Castle Terrace from behind the curtain. The line of parked cars had thinned out as the office building next door had emptied, and there were only three to be seen on the far side of the street, mine and two others, a battered old Mini and a Citroen with French plates. There was no sign of a policeman.

Jan and Prim looked at me anxiously as I came back into the kitchen. I answered them with a quick smile and a shake of the head. 'Whatever it was, he's buggered off.'

'That's good,' said Jan, 'because your rice must be nearly ready!'

We ate in the small back room which Noosh and Jan use as a dining room. The stir fry was one of Jan's best ever, full of chunky monkfish, mushrooms, yellow peppers and lemon grass, but it was wasted on me. I kept thinking about that copper, and his unhealthy interest in my car. I excused myself as soon as I had finished, and went back through to the living room, back to my stance behind the curtains.

The battered Mini was gone, but the Citroen was still there. Beyond it, there was a third car, a black Vauxhall Cavalier, with a mobile telephone antenna sticking out of its roof. There was a man in the driver's seat, a big man. It was still raining quite hard, and from that distance I couldn't quite make out his face, but I was in no doubt who it was.

I went back through to the dining room, where the girls were having coffee. 'Jan, have you still got that telescope?' I gave Jan a spyglass one Christmas, basically because I'd run out of ideas.

She looked puzzled for a second, than caught on. 'Yes. Come on.'

She led me through to the bedroom. The telescope was on her bedside table. In normal circumstances I'd have taken longer to wonder what they used it for, but my mind was on other things. Prim and Noosh were waiting for us in the living room. I motioned them to stay back from the window and slid in behind the curtain, taking care not to disturb it. Carefully I focused the telescope on the Cavalier. Just as I did so, the man in the driver's seat leaned forward, and I had a clear view of his face.

I swore softly.

'What is it?' asked Prim.

'It's Ricky Ross. That copper must have called in my number.'

Anoushka stood there looking bewildered. 'I'll tell you later,' Jan said to her.

'What are you going to do?' she asked.

193

'Good question. Is the washing machine finished drying out gear yet?'

'Should be.'

'Okay,' said Prim. 'I'll pack the bag.'

Jan stood in the centre of the room, mulling something over. At last she nodded, decisively. Then she kicked off her shoes, and ran back through to the bedroom, beckoning me to follow. By the time I got there she had stepped out of her skirt and was unbuttoning her blouse. 'What is this,' I said. 'One last time for luck?' I was comforted by the knowledge that even in times of crisis, the daft side of me could still come to the surface.

She shot me a quick, 'You should be so lucky!' and began to step into a pair of jeans which had been lying across the dressing-table stool. 'Get me your anorak,' she ordered. I began to see what she had in mind. I did as I was told and fetched the horrible, hooded green garment from the hall. She fastened her jeans and pulled on a sweatshirt, then tried the anorak for size. As I've said, she's a tall girl, so it wasn't a bad fit. She pulled on a pair of old trainers, looked at herself in a full-length mirror and nodded her satisfaction, then turned and pushed me out of the room, back into the kitchen. There, Prim was packing the final items into our bag, folding them as best she could. Noosh stood with her back to the sink, still looking bewildered.

'Right,' said Jan. 'This is your best chance. I'll wear this gear. I'll run out, jump into Oz's car and drive it away. I'll tie the hood tight, and with any luck, the guy out there will think it's Oz and follow.

'Oz, my Fiesta's parked in the back yard. Once you see him move off, the pair of you get downstairs and get as far away from here as you can. The car's not long after a service, so it

194

should get you to Switzerland all right.'

All of a sudden I was emotionally full up. I'd never felt closer to the girl; never in all of our lives had I realised how strong was the bond between us. 'Hold on a minute, Jan. This is a dangerous guy. He'll catch up with you.'

'But he won't stop me, not even if he lies down in the road. If I have to I'll just drive to the nearest police station and run in screaming that there's a man following me. Now no more arguments, unless you've got a better idea.'

I hadn't, and I didn't know what to ay, so I just kissed her. For a moment I thought Prim might be mad, but she kissed her too. Just to be on the safe side, I kissed Noosh as well. Prim drew the line at that.

Jan and I exchanged car keys, and we all went back through to the living room. We stood there in a circle, smiling nervously at each other. I tied the cords of the anorak hood tight under Jan's chin, pulling it down to cover her face. We shared a last long look that neither Noosh nor Prim could see, a look that said a hundred things, from 'Thanks' to 'Remember that time in the dunes in the East Bay at Elie, when there was no-one else around . . .' Probably, it was as well that neither Noosh nor Prim could see our eyes.

And then Jan was gone. The front door closed and she was off down the stairs. I went back to my spy-hole and looked down into the street. Every Tuesday at Meadowbank, Ali tells me I run like a girl, so she was a pretty good imitation. I didn't realise she could move that fast . . . well, she's never run away from me. She was across the street in a flash. Unlocking the door, she jumped into the car. Just then I panicked, thinking she'd flood the carburettor, but Jan knows the old Nissan pretty well, and it started first time.

As soon as I heard the engine's cough, I looked back at the

Cavalier. Ross was sitting bolt upright in his seat, fiddling with his key. I heard his ignition snarl, but soon it fired up. Jan had barely swung the Nissan away from the kerb and round into Johnstone Terrace, before he was after her. 'Clever girl,' I said. 'She'll lead him where there are no traffic lights.

'Right, let's do what she says, and make ourselves scarce. Thanks, Noosh, see you soon . . . we hope.'

I grabbed the bag with one hand and Prim with the other, and together we legged it down the stairs, past the front door and down to the basement level. Jan's red Fiesta Sport was next to the exit. It burst throatily into life at the first turn of the key. With barely a backward look we were off, out into Castle Terrace then away down to the Grassmarket, in the opposite direction to that in which Jan had headed.

Ali was waiting in the shop with our passports. Prim stayed in the car as I rushed in. 'Thanks mate,' I said. 'Do one thing more for me, will you. Get my diary and check my faxes and messages. Then call Jimmy and ask him to handle my work till I get back, same as usual.'

My chum nodded his turban. 'Fair enough. That still leaves one problem, though.'

'Eh?

'It means we'll be one short at the fitba' tomorrow night!'

In which we begin a circuitous journey South, and have a surprise phone call.

'So that's Jan's secret, is it?' Prim mused, as we headed down the A1, bypassing Haddington.

'No secret, except from the good burghers of Enster.'

'How long have they been . . .'

'I told you, around four years.'

'You should have said something to warn me, you sod. Mind you, when I saw that living room, I began to get the idea. It's a couple's room, but there's nothing masculine about it.' She thought about it some more. 'There's nothing stereotyped about them, is there?'

'No, they're not your average person's idea of a gay couple. But there's shades of everything you know.'

'They look happy enough. Are they, d'you think?'

'Most of the time. There are tensions, though.'

'Do you think it'll last?'

'I don't know. Look at the number of heterosexual relationships that break up. Why should gay couples be different? They have another complication too. Jan's AC/DC. Could be

197

she'll meet a man who can give her more than Noosh can. I hate to think how Anoushka'd cope with that.'

'Well, I think they're nice, and I hope she doesn't have to.'

'Okay, love, but just don't let Auntie Mary hear you say that.'

I drove on down the road towards the darkening South, taking care not to trip any of the speed cameras. I was still worried about Jan, being pursued by Ricky Ross, and I reckoned that the last thing she would want after that would be a fixed penalty speeding ticket, when she hadn't even been driving.

One of the good things about driving at night is the lack of heavy traffic. With nothing to hold us back, we made Newcastle in Jan's nippy wee motor in just under two hours.

'Oz,' said Prim, as the ring road round the city merged with the A1M, 'where exactly are we going? And do we have to get there in one go?'

She was right. I was just driving, with no clear game plan. 'I guess we're heading for Dover,' I said. 'I just want to get out of this country. Ross must have worked out what we've done by this time. Even if he didn't hassle Jan, by this time he'll know who she is. We've got to assume he's traced her car number through the police computer.'

'What if he has? What can he do about it? Will he have us stopped at the ferry?'

'Hardly. He can't involve anyone else in this or he's in trouble. I guess he'll come after us.'

'And when he finds us?' I wouldn't say that she sounded apprehensive, she never does. But the question was tentative, no doubt about it.

'Remember Willie Kane?' She nodded, getting my drift.

'Could he get ahead of us? Could he beat us to Dover?'

I thought about it. We'd wasted some time at Ali's, and if Ross had been able to do a quick PNC check, then . . . My musing was interrupted by the warbling of my mobile on the back seat. Even though I was driving, I jumped. Prim looked at me. I nodded to her. 'Answer it.'

She reached round, picking up the phone and pressed the receive button. 'Yes?' she said gruffly, disguising her voice, rather pointlessly I thought. Then her face lit up with relief. 'It's you, Jan! Are you okay?' She paused, listening. Suddenly she laughed. 'Serves him right. It was good of you to think of calling.

'Where are we?' She looked out of the window. 'Just passing Durham, I think. On our way to Dover, Oz says.

'Yes, of course. We'll try to keep in touch.' She pressed the cut-off button and put the phone on her lap.

'She's okay,' she said, sounding as relieved as I was. 'Apparently he didn't get alongside her until red traffic lights at Meadowbank. When he looked across, she just pulled the hood down and glared at him. She said she thought he would burst.

'He signalled her to pull over and she did, because there were plenty of people around. He asked her who she was and she told him. Then she asked him what he meant by this. He spun her a story about you being under police observation on suspicion of theft. She said that was rubbish. She said your father was a dentist, as if that would help!

'She told him that you were out of town and that you'd lent her your car since hers was being repaired. Then she got stroppy with him and asked to see his warrant card. That was enough. He said, "Sorry to have troubled you, Miss," and buggered off.'

I winced. 'Thank Christ she's okay. I doubt if Ross'll give

her any more trouble. Still, he has her name. That means he'll have all the rest of it by now.'

I looked at the clock on the dashboard. If it was accurate, it was twenty to ten.

'Tell you what,' I said. 'Why don't we stop for the night? Ross might not be able to catch us before we reach Dover, but he could get there before the ferry sailed.'

'Couldn't we take the Chunnel?'

I made a face. 'I hate Chunnels. Anyway, the same thing could happen there. No, here's my suggestion. We stop now for the night. Tomorrow we drive to Portsmouth and take a ferry to Brittany. Then we head across France and surprise my big sister. She and her man live near the Swiss border.

'If Ross is following us, he's bound to head for Dover, then for Geneva and Berners Bank, just as fast as he can. Let him. If we don't go there ourselves until next Thursday, maybe, by that time, he'll have decided we're not coming.'

'Some chance of that!' I thought.

'Some chance of that!' Prim said. 'But yes, I'll buy that idea. We might as well travel in comfort. Let Ross do the chasing!'

We turned off at Darlington, but as an added precaution, we decided not to stop in one of the hotels in town. Instead we headed for the outskirts, until we came upon a place not big enough to call itself a village, appropriately named Middleton-One-Row. It was big enough to have a nice road-side inn, the kind that's always popular with reps. There was one room left, twin-bedded. I looked at Prim, questioningly. She nodded, so I booked us in. The owner was a cheerful chap, and his chef did a remarkably good salmon *en croûte*, even at that time of night. Afterwards, we had a couple of pints with our host. His name was Peter and he seemed glad of the

200

company, but at a quarter to midnight, we said goodnight and left him to close up.

Our room was nicely furnished, with a real *en suite* bathroom, not one of those partitioned-off jobs in the corner, the kind in which you try to pee quietly so your partner won't hear.

We lay side by side on our twin beds, each of us staring up at the ceiling. 'My brain's still travelling at 100 miles an hour,' said Prim. 'What a day this has been! Pure mayhem!'

I propped myself up on an elbow and gazed across at her. 'Do you have any other kind? It occurs to me that since I met you, my feet have hardly touched the ground.'

'I don't know about that,' she said, pushing herself off her divan and coming to join me on mine, 'but I do know that this will be the fourth different bed that I've slept in in the last five nights.'

I thought about that one, reached behind her, under her shirt, and unclipped her bra, one-handed. 'True. It's a bit like the Grand Prix circuit, isn't it. D'you think we should start giving them marks out of ten?'

She unzipped me and eased her hand inside my jeans. There wasn't much room in there any more. 'Not *them*, Osbert,' she whispered '*Us*. I reckon it's time for a test drive.' She leaned over me, pinning me down, and kissed me, disengaging herself with difficulty from my Levis, and going to work on the buckle of my belt.

'There is one thing, though,' she said, as I began to ease her out of her clothes. 'I've been off the pill for two years, and being a nurse, I know about cycles. Right now, if you even point that thing at me, I could get pregnant. So I hope that with all these propositions you've been throwing at me, you're carrying a supply.'

201

My face fell, just a second before hers. 'Christ,' she laughed. 'Nineties man!'

'Meets Sixties woman!' I retorted.

We lay there, half-undressed, shaking our heads and laughing, until Prim jumped up, half out of her tights, and hopped back across to her bed. She was almost there when I had a brainwave.

'Hold on, this is a reps' hotel. The Gents is bound to have a slot machine.'

We rifled through our change until we found four pound coins. Silently, I padded downstairs to the gents' toilet off the hallway. My heart rose as I saw the machine on the wall. It fell again, just as quickly.

Peter's is a popular hotel with reps; but just as popular, it seems, are the reps who use it. The machine was in perfect working order. It was also perfectly empty.

In which we plan to score
high marks on the high seas
but end up cast adrift.

'I wonder where Ricky Ross is waking up,' Prim said, as she stretched luxuriously, arching her back and squeezing the last of the sleep out of her body. She's the best str-e-e-e-tcher I've ever seen. When she does it she looks like a lioness, with her blonde mane and her golden skin.

'I hope the bastard's been driving all right,' I said, 'and that right about now he drops off to sleep at the wheel and totals himself.' I really meant it, and it must have sounded that way too, for Prim looked at me in surprise.

'If only life was that simple,' she said. She propped herself up on an elbow and grinned across at me. 'What's the game plan for today, lover-boy? Want to look around the shops this morning before we head south. Like Boots, maybe?'

'I could nip out now, if you like,' I said, experimentally.

She snorted. 'The Grant Prix circuit's closed. What time's breakfast?' I looked at my watch. It was almost quarter past nine.

'We've got about fifteen minutes to get down there.'

Prim showered while I shaved, and so we were able to make it with about five seconds to spare. We both felt guilty about keeping the chef from his break, so we settled for cereal and coffee.

Peter, it seemed, had taken to us. He was sorry to see us go, but Prim cheered him up when she said we'd look in on the way back. I muttered that when we did, all the facilities had better be in working order. He stared at me for a few seconds, until at last he grasped my meaning. 'Ah,' he said, mournfully, 'that's the trouble with outside suppliers.'

Rather than head south straight away we drove back into Darlington. It's a nice town, distinctive, with a market in its centre set out around a high tower. After I'd been to Boots, we found a travel agent and looked up ferry times from the south coast ports. 'I've never seen St Malo,' I suggested. The travel agent assured us that there would be plenty of space on a night crossing in midweek, so that was it.

We had nine hours to get to Portsmouth, and we used them all, driving at a steady pace, bypassing Leeds and circling south of Birmingham till we found the M40. We chatted as we travelled, when we weren't singing along to Jan's Abba tapes. (The woman's never been the same since she saw *Muriel's Wedding*.) We tried to talk about the future, but for both of us the crystal ball was obscured by the dark shadow of Ricky Ross, and our task in Geneva.

'If you've finished with nursing, honey,' I asked Prim as we crawled through Newbury, 'what are you going to do? Not, I say again, that you need to do anything.'

She shook her head, then shrugged her shoulders. 'I don't know, I really don't. All I do know is that I have to do something, but it has to be something really different.'

'How about marrying me and having babies?' The words

204

jumped unbidden from my mouth. I twisted the mirror and stared in it to make sure that it was me who had said them.

'Woah, Oz, woah,' she said. 'All in good time. It's only been five days, and we haven't even had that test drive yet. Your application still has to be approved.'

I must have looked downcast, because she squeezed my thigh. 'A couple of years down the road, if we can still stand each other, then we can talk about things like that. But is that what you really want?'

I took a hand off the wheel and stroked her soft cheek. 'Right now, Springtime, what I want is you. Anything else is a bonus.

'Tell you what, let's get the next few days over with. If we're still alive in a week, we'll have the rest of our lives in front of us!'

We drove on in silence for a while. Talk of test drives, and our developing, if frustrating, relationship made me think about ferry crossings. Jan and I went to London once. There's something about making love in a British Rail sleeper. I wondered if it might be the same on a cross-channel ferry. My Dad's house has cupboards that are bigger than railway sleepers but those narrow berths were an experience . . . especially with both of us crammed into the lower one.

We got to Portsmouth with two hours to spare. The travel agent was right, up to a point. There was plenty of vehicle space, with no buses booked on board. But there were absolutely no spare cabins. I looked at Prim as we stood at the booking window. 'Am I being punished for something?' I asked her. 'Are you? Has your Mum had a word with the Bloke Upstairs?'

In terms of Grand Prix circuits, the Club Class lounge on a Channel Ferry is strictly a pedestrian precinct.

205

We sat side by side in our reclining aircraft-style seats, the Fetherlites redundant in my wallet, and held hands through the night, all the way to France.

In which we arrive on a movie set and thwart a daring escape bid.

I like motoring in France. I don't know my left from my right at the best of times, so driving on the 'wrong' side of the road is no big deal for me.

There is this theory that to get to anywhere in France from the Channel ports you have to go through Paris. It's rubbish, of course. We hung about in St Malo for a while, just to get the feel of it, then headed south to Rennes. Using a map which we'd bought at the terminal we plotted a route more or less alongside the Loire, until we picked up the Autoroute which led to Lyon.

We made a couple of stops along the way, and Prim gave me yet another surprise. I may like France, but when it comes to speaking the language, I'm about as useful as Harpo Marx. Prim turned out to be fluent. 'It was Africa,' she explained. 'French was the main language where I was, so I had to pick it up.'

The day grew hotter as we went further south, until the information signs along the road were showing an outside temperature of 28 degrees. To make it tolerable we drove with the windows down and the sunroof open, but even at that, touching the steering wheel felt a bit like handling hot bread straight from the oven.

'Where does your sister live?' Prim asked as we pulled into a service area, to make another pit stop, and to buy food to take to Ellen's. Arriving empty-handed is not the done thing in the Blackstone family.

'A place called Pérrouges. I've never been there, but she says it's nice. Sort of old, she says.'

We found it without too much trouble, but when we got there we could barely believe our eyes. It turned out that my sister's home is in a piece of living history, a walled townlet with cobbled streets narrow enough to offer shade nearly all day, and hardly a building that's less than two hundred and fifty years old.

'Jesus,' said Prim. 'It's a movie set!'

Naturally, I'd forgotten to bring a note of Ellen's address, but my tour guide solved the problem by going into the town's tiny hotel and asking the receptionist where the Scots family lived. It wasn't far – nowhere in Pérrouges is far – just round the corner and down a twisty alley.

We knew the house before we got there. When they handed out the lungs, our Ellen was right up at the front of the queue.

'Jonathan!' The shout seemed to fill the narrow alleyway, bouncing back and forth off the stone walls. I jumped. It was pure reflex. When I was a kid, Ellen's bellow could freeze my blood from two hundred yards away. Close up it could emasculate an elephant. The sound was still echoing, on its way, no doubt, to frighten distant wildlife, when my older nephew came diving head first out of a low window, about thirty feet away. He did a perfect rolling landing, winding up on his feet, and kick-started a sprint. His trainers threw up puffs of dust as he raced up the sloping pathway towards us. He made to shimmy round us, head down, but I grabbed his shoulder. At first he tried to wriggle out of my grasp, and only when he found it was too strong for him, did he look up.

'Hello there, Wee Man. What have you been up to then?'

His mouth dropped open, answering my question in the process. It, and half of his face, was stained by the juice of berries.

'Uncle Oz! Uncle Oz!' He was so surprised that he forgot all about his escape bid, and his predicament. 'Mum, Mum!' he shouted, back down the alley. 'See who's here! See who's here!' Jonathan is only just turned seven, but he's showing signs already that he's inherited his mother's lung-power. I let him go and he ran back to the house, crashing through the door this time, rather than the window. A second or two later there was the sharp, unmistakable 'Splat!' of palm on bare leg, and a second after that the sound of a howl being stifled as Jonathan gasped out his news through the string of retribution.

'If you're making up stories again . . .' said Ellen as she stepped outside.

It had been over a year since I'd seen her. The first thing I realised was that there was more of her to see. Ellen's always been a square-built sort of girl, but France had straightened out what curves she had. I wouldn't say she'd got fat . . . no, to be honest, I would. She'd got fat.

She stared at me. 'Oz, you *bugger*! You might have let me know!' Jonathan appeared again by her side, sniffling and smiling at the same time, pulling his wee brother Colin along behind him.

I gave her a bear-sized hug. It's only when I see Ellen after a break that I realise how much she means to me. She hugged me back and looked up at me. If it had been anyone but Ellen, I'd have said there was a tear in the corner of her eye.

'Hi, Sis. I know we should have called, but it was a spur of the moment thing. Ellie, this is Prim Phillips, my girlfriend.'

You know right away how my sister feels about someone. If she has doubts, it shows in a narrowing of her eyes that she doesn't even know is there. She looked at Primavera, wide-eyed, and grinned. I have to say that even after a day's drive through France, Prim looked fantastic. The sun had given her skin an extra glow, and had picked out shiny highlights in her hair.

'You poor lassie,' said Ellen, 'come on in.'

The house was fantastic. Not huge, but big enough for a young family. It had a stone floor and walls, which made it wonderfully cool, and beamed ceilings, yet the important parts were modern. The kitchen, to which we followed Ellen, was lined with hand-built cupboards, and fitted out with every available appliance. A Pyrex bowl sat on the work-surface, half full of strawberries. Around it there lay piles of green husks.

Ellen pointed at it, still outraged. 'See that wee so-and-so. They were for tonight.' She glowered at her older son. 'So help me God!' Jonathan, reckoning he was on safer ground with me around, chanced his arm by smiling.

'It's all right, Ellie,' I said. 'We've got some more in the car.' I cuffed Jonathan, very lightly, around the ear. 'None for you though, pal.'

'Allan still at work?' I asked, innocently, and was concerned to see a shadow cross her face.

'Of course,' she said. 'Allan works every hour God sends. Allan volunteers for extra work. Last week he was away so early and home so late that he didn't see his kids at all.' She tried to sound casual, but she didn't fool me. My sister was not a happy lady.

I didn't want to get into the domestics, so I changed the subject. 'How are you getting on with the language?'

'Bloody awful,' she said. 'Stuff that, though. How's Dad?'

'He's great. I might as well tell you straight off; he's got a new interest in life. Auntie Mary.'

Ellen's face lit up again. 'That's great. I've been hoping that would happen. And how about Jan? Is she still with the German?' Ellen did not approve of Jan's relationship.

'Slovakian, Sis. She's Slovakian. Aye, they're still going strong.'

'And you two. How long have you been . . .'

We were still talking in the kitchen when Allan came in a couple of hours later, just after nine, but by that time the kids were in bed, our kit was in the spare room, and a meal had been prepared. '*Coq au Vin*' Ellen called it, muttering something about 'shaggin' in a Transit', but it looked like chicken in red wine sauce to me.

I try to make excuses for my brother-in-law, especially to my Dad, but I always wind up admitting that he's a selfish, boring get. Allan is not the sort of guy you'd invite out to the pub. He was surprised to see us, of course, but not the sort of surprise that gives way to a big smile, like Ellen's did. He barely hid his irritation at our disruption of his routine.

We ate outside in their small courtyard. Ellie asked Prim about Africa, and to be polite, I asked Allan about his job. He gave me a lecture on the state of the oil industry; I told him that I always judged the state of the oil industry by the number of rigs tied up idle in the Firth of Forth. Finally, as soon as half-decent manners allowed, my brother-in-law offered the 'early start' excuse and went upstairs.

211

Later, as Prim and I undressed in the tiny guest room, we thought we heard the sound of my sister's raised voice. 'See if I ever get like him, sweetheart,' I said. 'Make sure you shoot me before you leave, will you.'

In which an unhappy sister
lends us her car and
plots her own escape.

We decided that French Grand Prix should be postponed until another night.

Neither of us said anything, but we knew that it just wouldn't have been right in that unhappy house, under that roof. Instead, we lay together in the big iron-framed bed which almost filled the room, Prim in her nightshirt, me in my boxers, making our plans for the last stage of our journey, and trying not to dwell on the danger which might be lying in wait for us.

Next morning, when I wandered downstairs at seven o'clock for a glass of water, Allan was gone.

Over breakfast, with Jonathan packed off to school and Colin sent into the courtyard with a bun and a football, Ellen tried to keep her brave face on it, and I tried to go along with it. But it was no use.

'What is it, Ellie?' I asked her. 'D'you feel homesick, or what?'

She shook her head. 'No, wee brither. I feel bored. I feel

uncared for. I feel abandoned. Try to imagine what it's like living here. The place is lovely, sure, but so what. It's in the middle of nowhere, the natives are unfriendly. Bloody Hell, the place even has a wall round it. It's a place to visit, not to live, and yet I'm stuck here full-time with nothing to do but eat pastries and go quietly out of my mind. Look at the size of me, Oz. I'm like a bloody bus.

'How would you fancy this for a life? How would you, Prim?' Prim rolled her big eyes, and shook her head, solemnly.

'But Ellie,' I said, 'shouldn't you have thought all this out before you bought the place?'

She glared at me. 'I didn't buy it, brother. Allan did. He took the job, the company came up with this and he said okay. You don't think he consulted me about any of it, do you!'

I watched her as she savaged her third croissant. 'You know what, Ellie?' I said. 'I reckon that's mostly shite. You were brought up in Anstruther, for heaven's sake. That's hardly a bloody metropolis. Yet you could handle that, and, if everything else was okay, you could handle this.

'But we both know that right now, if you were living in the middle of the Champ d'Elysée, you'd still be bored out of your tree, and we both know why.'

But she wasn't ready for such fundamental truth. She shook her head and stood up, to fetch more coffee from the big range cooker. 'Enough about me,' she said, sitting back down at the table.

'Are you going to tell me, finally, what it is that's brought you two out here? And don't say you just came on holiday. You're a creature of habit, Oz. You take your holidays in July, like the rest of Scotland.'

Normally, Ellie's the third person in the world, alongside my Dad and Jan, that I'd have trusted with our problem. But all of a sudden I wasn't sure. She had problems of her own.

'Are you working up to telling me something bad about Dad?' she probed.

I shook my head. 'No, not at all. It's nothing like that. Look if I told you you'd think I'm mad.'

She looked me dead in the eye. 'Oz, remember when we were kids? Who did you come to when you were in bother? And who sorted it out for you? As for being mad, what's new?

'So come on boy. Out with it.'

So, just as I had with Jan and my Dad, I told her. I left out not a scrap of detail, from the size of Willie Kane's organ, to the size of his wife's betrayal. When I had finished, my sister was smiling. 'It's just like when you were Jonathan's age.

'You know, Prim, this bugger never got into ordinary bother like other kids. He did it in the grand style. I remember one summer: the man next door grew garden peas, on stalks, and they were right up against the boundary fence. This yin here, he reached through the fence, and he stripped all the peas out of nearly all the pods, but left them hanging there. When the man's wife went out to pick her peas, all she found was empty pods, hangin' there looking pathetic, like blown green condoms. There was hell to pay. He'd maybe have got away with it too, only he kept the evidence in a basin in his room!'

All of a sudden she was serious. 'Are you sure you're right about this man Ross?'

'As sure as we can be.'

'And you can't go to the police?'

I shook my head. 'He *is* the police. We'd wind up in the nick ourselves, and my client's business would be bust. There is the other angle too.'

'What's that?'

'If we can avoid Ross, and get the money back to Archer,

we collect ten per cent commission. That's ninety thousand, Ellie.'

'I'm a teacher. I had worked that out!' She shot me her old familiar glower. Everything was all right again.

'So you reckon that Ross'll have come after you.'

'Sure. He isn't just after ten per cent. He's after the lot.'

'So what's your next step? Geneva?'

I nodded.

'Right. If he's there he'll be looking out for Jan's car. So you two take mine. Just you drive right up to the door of the bank and march straight in. Once you've got the money, don't come back here. Head north. I'll take Jan's car back. It's time the kids saw their Grandad again.'

'What will Allan say about that?'

She looked at me, and it was as if I was back in the school playground. 'Not a bloody word, unless he wants his legs slapped!'

In which we cross the border and reach our objective.

Ellen's car was a farty wee Peugeot diesel, so short of horsepower that when the air conditioning clicked on, you felt a 'clunk', and the beast slowed by about five miles an hour. But it *had* air conditioning, and on the baking Autoroute as we headed for the Swiss border, that was real consolation for the loss of Jan's nippy wee Fiesta.

It isn't very far from the east side of Lyon to Switzerland, barely as much as an hour, even in Ellen's clunker. It was still morning when we crossed the border. I'd never been in Switzerland before, but I had seen Swiss drivers in action on the Autoroutes, and so I was extra careful.

We pulled into the first parking area we could find, to study the street map of Geneva that we had bought back in France. The place looked a bit smaller than Edinburgh. I was pleased, because it meant that Berners Bank should be relatively easy to find, but concerned, because I figured that the smaller the place, the easier we'd be to find.

Dawn had told us that the bank was more or less in the city

centre, in a street which bore its name. We found the index on the back of our map, and sure enough, there it was, Rue Berner, grid reference H6.

If Lyon is only a stone's throw from Switzerland, Geneva is only a spit from the border. We had hardly started down the road before the countryside was giving way to built-up areas. As we descended, in the distance we could see, beyond the city, the blue water of Lake Geneva, and beyond that the towering massif of Mont Blanc.

The first thing that struck me about Geneva was the flags. I don't think I've ever seen as many flagpoles in my life, or as many colours flying upon them. It's a real international city, just as much as London or Paris, and in some ways even more so. After all, the Red Cross is based there, and the World Health Organisation, and even, I read once, the World Council of Churches. *Appropriate*, I thought, feeling the stirring of my Calvinist roots.

Prim navigated us smoothly along the broad green avenues, taking left, then right, then right again. We missed Rue Berner first time around, but a laborious loop brought us into it at last. It was a big, wide street, with two-way traffic, and very definitely no parking. We drove down it as slowly as we could, shrinking into our seats as we looked around for any sign of Ricky Ross, but seeing none.

Berners was about four hundred yards down the street, its name picked out in beaten copper on a sign above a dark, narrow doorway. 'There it is,' said Prim, her voice hushed but excited. 'Do you see him?' she asked.

'No sign of him, as far as I can see.'

'What'll we do with the car?'

At that moment, I didn't have a clue, but just then the answer presented itself, a big blue 'P' sign above a doorway a hundred yards ahead. I swung the car in, took a ticket from an automatic machine and found myself steering sharply down and round a spiralling ramp which opened out eventually into a long neon-lit garage. We found a space, parked and just sat there, our hearts pounding, breathing heavily.

'This is it,' I said, trying to sound confident, but, I'm sure, sounding scared instead. 'Ten minutes and it'll be done.'

Prim nodded. 'Or we will,' she said, brightly. I didn't need to be reminded of that.

'There's still time to back out,' I said, quickly, to myself as much as to her. But I knew there wasn't. Sometimes, a man has to do . . . and all that. To steel myself, I thought ahead, of what it would be like when the thing was over, and Archer had the money back, and Prim and I could get down to some serious living together.

'Okay,' I said, at last, my loins as girded up as they were going to get. 'Let's go and get Archer's cash.'

Prim drew me to her, and kissed me. I could feel her hands trembling very slightly. 'I love you, Oz Blackstone,' she said, for the first time. 'Nothing can stop you and me.'

'I love you too, Primavera,' I said, grinning like an idiot, 'and you know what? I think you're right.'

She reached into her handbag, fiddled with her purse, and pulled out half of a five pound note. 'You'll need this.' I read the serial number aloud, 'AF 426469. Remember, that's the number of the account too.'

Apart from the map, we'd picked up a few other things in France. On the basis that even the most basic disguise might help, we'd bought floppy sun-hats, blue for me, white for Prim, and Vuarnet sun-glasses, a good brand that were going to cost Ray Archer plenty on my expense account. Finally, realising just in time that nine hundred thousand sterling might be just a shade bulky, we'd found a good size duffel bag. It was still stuffed with waste-paper packing, and we decided to leave it that way, looking full, so that out on the street we'd look even more like a couple of plonker tourists.

There was a lift up from the garage, to a narrow glazed door which opened directly out on to Rue Berner. We peered through the glass. Outside, the pavements on either side of the street were thronged, with business people rather than tourists. This was a commercial centre, with nothing to attract sightseers. We pulled on our sun-hats, then our shades.

'We should have taken the ones with the false noses and moustaches,' said Prim, giggling, very slightly nervously, but looking, I thought proudly to myself, absolutely sensational in tee-shirt and shorts. We looked at each other for reassurance and, taking a deep breath, stepped outside.

In which we do the business
and Berner rings the bell.

The air was a lot cooler than it had been in Pérrouges, even in the morning. As the business people bustled by us, some of them in fairly heavy clothing, we realised all of a sudden how out of place we looked.

'Come on,' I said, picking up the pace until I was almost at a trot. Those last few yards to Berners were the most nervous of my life. Every step I took, I was tensed for a shout, or a heavy hand on my shoulder.

But nothing happened. Unimpeded, we reached the narrow entrance to the bank and almost fell inside. We took off our redundant sunglasses and hats and stuffed them into the duffel bag.

When I think of a bank, I think of a line of tellers behind counters, usually in a high-domed airy hall, where every whisper about the sad state of my account carries to the inquisitive ears of everyone else in the room.

I'd heard the term 'private bank' before. I even know of one in Edinburgh. But until I set foot in Berners I had no idea what the term really meant. There was a short hallway off the street, with an unmarked door, closed, to the right and a second door at the end, opening and welcoming. We stepped inside. For a second I had the strangest feeling, that somehow I was back in my Dad's front room. The furniture was similar, of the same vintage, and arranged in much the same way, around a fireplace, with an embroidered screen in front, not unlike my Mum's. The only major difference was a big rosewood desk, set before the curtained window.

We stared at each other. The room was empty. We looked around for a bell, something to ring, and call 'Shop!'

We didn't see a camera, but it must have been there, because when the door in the far wall opened and the man stepped in, he was smiling a greeting before he'd even seen us. He stretched out a hand and said, 'Good Day'; or rather, he said, 'Bonjour'.

'*Oh shit*,' I thought, but Prim shook his hand, returned his smile, and said simply, '*En Anglais, s'il vous plaît*.'

'Of course,' said the banker. He was a tall thin bloke, grey-haired, with a complexion that was so sallow it was virtually cream-coloured.

'I am Jean Berner. How can I help you?' I had the strangest feeling that he knew the answer already.

'We wish to make a cash withdrawal,' said Prim, 'from numbered account AF 426469. I believe that these represent the key.' She took out her half of the fiver from her purse. I unbuttoned my shirt pocket and produced the other half.

Berner took the two pieces of banknote from her and checked each number. 'That is correct,' he said. 'But you are not the young lady who opened the account.'

'No,' said Prim. 'That was my sister. But the arrangement was that possession of the note gives the bearers authority to operate it.'

He nodded. 'Of course. How much would you wish to withdraw?'

'Nine hundred thousand pounds, sterling,' I said.

Berner stepped over to the desk, produced a key, unlocked a central drawer and took out a sheaf of computer printouts. It looked completely out of place in that room as he leafed through it. 'But that will leave a balance of only forty-eight thousand,' he said. 'Our minimum deposit level is fifty thousand in sterling.' I looked at him, astonished. Even allowing for interest on the lump sum, Wee Willie must have salted away at least another thirty K that no-one knew about.

'In that case, close the account, please,' said Prim. 'We'll withdraw it all.'

If I was a banker and someone came in and told me that I'd lost a private account worth nearly a million squigglies, I'd be pissed off up to my neckline. Jean Berner's smug half-smile never wavered. I found myself wondering whether he regarded sterling as second-class money, and was glad to be shot of it.

'You will wait here, please.' He oiled his way back through the door, still carrying the printouts and Prim's fiver.

As the door closed behind him, Prim gave a wee jump of joy. I thought she was going to shout out loud, and somehow, with a video camera in the room, I didn't want that to happen. So I caught her in mid-jump and pulled her to me in a hug. She looked at me surprised, and gave me her most delicious grin. 'We're . . .'

I kissed her, to stop her mouth. 'We're on Candid Camera in here, so careful what you say and do.'

Still she smiled. 'Wow,' she whispered. 'You really are paranoid. He's gone to get our money, Oz. Relax.'

'When we step out of Ray Archer's office with our ten per cent, partner, then I'll relax,' I whispered back. 'Until then, this is just too easy, and he's just too pleased with himself.'

We stood there, hugging and kissing, and throwing in the odd bump and grind for the cameras.

Berner returned in a shade under five minutes, carrying a canvas satchel and an A4 form. And the bugger was still smiling. He put the bag on the desk and opened it wide for us to see inside. 'There you are,' he said. 'Nine hundred and forty-eight thousand pounds sterling. Now if you will each sign this withdrawal form . . .'

'Count it, please,' I said, really niggled by that smile. He looked at me, as if he was disappointed in me.

'But M'sieur, this is a reputable Swiss bank.'

'Oui, M'sewer,' I said. 'And I am a suspicious Scots bastard! Indulge us.'

With the sigh he would give to an awkward child, Berner unpacked all the money from the bag and piled it on the desk. There were nine large bundles and one smaller one. 'This money is in Bank of England fifty pound notes,' he said, picking up one of the larger bundles. 'Each one of these contains one hundred thousand pounds. He riffled through the bundle, holding it up for us to see. I worked out how thick two thousand fifty pound notes should be and nodded. He riffled through each of the others in turn, showing us that there was no newsprint laced in there. Not that I thought for a moment there would be. I just wanted to do something, anything to rile the guy. No chance. He was still smiling when he finished his riffling. He began to pack the satchel once more. Our wee duffel bag looked pretty silly beside it. When he was finished, he clicked its catch shut and snapped a small padlock into place. As we signed the form he produced a key, and held it out to Prim, together with the two halves of her fiver.

'Thank you very much,' he said. 'I hope that one day your

organisation will do business with Berners again.' We looked at him, puzzled. My old friend the hamster started running around in my stomach.

'Now for your surprise,' said Berner. 'You do not have to go to Lausanne to meet your colleague. He is here.' He reached under the rosewood desk and pressed a button. We heard a bell ring.

'Come on love,' I said picking up the heavy bag and taking Prim by the hand. 'Let's quit this town.'

Without an 'au revoir' to Berner we headed out of the room towards the exit. But the small door off the hall was open, and the hall wasn't empty any more. It was full: full of Rawdon Brooks.

In which Hansel and Gretel
are right up against
it in the forest.

He stood there, wrists limp no longer; instead he was tall, surprisingly wide-shouldered, narrow-waisted, and very trim in a beautifully cut jacket. There was no trace at all of the effete character we had met in the Lyceum rehearsal room. This Rawdon Brooks looked very dangerous, and I had no doubt at all that he was.

'So you made it at last, little people,' he said in a fruity, friendly voice, loud enough for Berner to hear through the open door. 'Come on and I'll tell you about the change of plan.' He was dressed immaculately, grey slacks accompanying his jacket. Again I flashed back to our first meeting, and realised what a consummate actor the man was. *'Which is the real him?'* I asked myself, until I saw the answer in his eyes.

His hands were clasped together in front of him, with an overcoat draped over them. He flicked the coat to one side, letting us see the silenced gun. After that we weren't about to argue. Her jerked his head towards the door. Prim, white-faced, walked past him and opened it, and we stepped out into the street.

All that stuff about being safe in a crowd, God, what rubbish that is. Brooks stepped close behind us and dug the gun into my back. 'Right,' he said in a voice that, suddenly, wasn't at all friendly. 'Walk in front of me, Oz. Primavera, take his arm. Now young man, remember this. You do just one thing wrong, and she gets it first, then you. Now do as I say. Walk!'

I could tell he wasn't in a negotiating mood. I walked, with Prim holding my arm, keeping the leisurely pace of a tourist, making certain that I didn't do *anything* wrong. He walked in silence until we reached the end of Rue Berner. 'Turn left,' said Rawdon. We did as we were told. All of a sudden, the pavement was even more crowded, but narrower. Brooks moved up alongside me. 'Right, Miss Phillips,' he said. 'Now it's the other way around. You do anything wrong and Oz gets it first, then you.

'Now we're going down this road until the next traffic lights, then we cross.'

As we walked, I realised that something strange had happened. The hamster wasn't running around in my stomach any more. Instead it felt as if it was encased in a block of ice. I had passed way beyond plain scared; now I knew what truly terrified felt like. I think I may have spoken to him to stop myself from passing out. 'Tell us, Rawdon,' I said. 'What tale did you spin Berner?'

He laughed, but it was as cold as his voice. There was triumph in it, triumph over me, triumph over Prim. He had my girl and me in his power and suddenly I hated him for it. Truly, I'd never hated anyone in my life before. The ice began to melt. Something I had been told years before by a soldier pal came back to me. 'Anger overcomes fear.' It doesn't, but it helps. I concentrated on my hatred as hard as I could.

'That was so easy,' he said, maddeningly self-confident. 'One is an actor after all. It's one's job to make people believe. I told him that I was a policeman on an Interpol operation with two Special Branch colleagues. We were off to pay off an informer who'd helped us round up some terrorists. I told him that the money was in the account that poor little Kane used dear Dawn to set up.

'I said that I'd travelled down first, and that you two would come down later with the banknote, pick up the cash and then rendezvous with me in a hotel in Lausanne. Only your car had broken down on the way, and I wasn't sure when you'd arrive, so I'd cancelled the hotel in Lausanne and come to meet you at the bank.

'I arranged with Berner to give you a little surprise. He'd allow me to wait in his anteroom until you two arrived, then when you'd done our business, he'd press his bell and I'd appear out of nowhere. It worked a treat, didn't it! One of my better productions, I'd say. It certainly gave my audience a start.'

Suddenly it all came back to me, what Dawn had said about him, and the College of Cardinals. 'Willie Kane cried it all out on your shoulder, didn't he. At the theatre club. He told you what he'd done for Dawn, about the bank account, about the money he'd stolen, about the key. Gay men are such good listeners after all, aren't you!'

We had reached the traffic lights, and the crossing indicator was flashing. 'Go on,' he said digging me in the ribs with the gun. 'Right,' he said, once we were on the other side of the street, 'that's where we're going, to that park down there. So we can decide what to do with you.' He added that as an afterthought, but we both knew that he'd made up his mind.

'You really are a good detective, Oz,' he said. He was

229

rubbing his power into us now, the bastard. 'That's just what happened.'

'But how did you get into Prim's flat? When I phoned, it was a woman who answered.'

He laughed softly. 'Did you really think so?' I thought back. A high voice. An arch tone. But in hindsight, no, not feminine: effeminate.

'Poor little Willie. When Dawn told him it couldn't go on he was distraught. He had stolen the money by that time. Even if he had given it back, his career would have been over. If he'd gone back to that wife of his, she'd have torn out his fingernails as a punishment.' He paused.

'She was there, you know, on the night. Just as I parked my car she came out, looking furious, having given the errant husband one last piece of her mind.

'The little chap asked me to come and see him, you know. He hadn't a clue what he wanted any more. So I persuaded him that he needed something new, something different. I told him to get undressed, lie down, and close his eyes, and that I'd make everything all right.' He laughed, an awful cold sound. 'And didn't I just.'

Geneva, they say, is famous for its parks, and the one towards which we were heading was probably its biggest, with a wide grassy area leading up to thick woodland. It was the middle of the afternoon, and for all its size it was uncomfortably empty. The forest seemed to go on for ever, and it looked very dark indeed. I suspected that on the other side there was nothing but the lake, since, above the tree-line, I could see the spume of the great Geneva fountain. All in all, it didn't look like the sort of place where you'd want to go with a man with a gun. But we had no choice: Brooks shoved us roughly through the gates.

'But you didn't find the fiver, Rawdon, did you?' I said, as we stumbled towards the woods.

'No indeed. Hard as I looked. And I never would, but for the strangest piece of luck. The very next night, dear PC McArthur came to the club. He was actually smiling! Unusual for him. I asked him what the joke was, and he said that his inspector was in terrible trouble because he had allowed a witness to take a piece of evidence away from a murder scene. A five pound note he said. A young couple, he said.

'And then, the morning after, you come barging into the Lyceum, all bright-eyed and full of investigative zeal. I had the whole picture then.'

We were more than halfway across the grass, nearing the woods. 'That policeman who questioned you before us,' said Prim. 'He never existed, did he?'

Brooks laughed. 'Of course not. Just a little something to set you off a-worrying about little sister.

'Once I knew you had the note, I knew that eventually, you'd wind up here. With the company in recess, it was just a matter of coming down here and waiting. Although I did think you'd have got here sooner.'

'So what happens now?' asked Primavera, direct as always. It was a question I'd been avoiding.

'Ferry crossings are really insecure things, you know,' said Brooks. 'You can take an unlicensed gun abroad in a car without worrying about being searched. You can even take really high quality heroin through, and a hypodermic.'

'*A bit of a junkie*,' Dawn had said. 'So that's it.' I think I may have snarled at him. 'We're going to have an overdose.' A picture flashed, unbidden into my mind: that poor dead lassie from years back, in that close, with me, in uniform, on guard at its mouth. I could see her, as clear as day.

231

'Precisely. You'll just be another couple of dead addicts. And when they find you, sooner or later, there'll be nothing to identify you. I think there are foxes in there too.'

We had reached the woods. 'Right, Hansel and Gretel, hold hands and go on ahead. But don't forget the gun.'

He drove us on through the trees, like animals. It grew darker and darker in there, with no sign of the other side. The traffic noise was distant, too. No, this was no copse, this was an urban forest.

At last we saw an area up ahead, where the trees seemed to thin, and where more light was allowed in from above. 'Enough,' said Brooks. 'This'll do. Now: Oz, dear boy, drop the bag. Then, both of you, turn around.'

We did as we were told. The big bastard just stood there, smiling at us, almost laughing. It was the way he was enjoying it, that was what was working on me. He was going to kill Prim, and he was looking forward to it.

He threw his raincoat on the ground and reached into the side pocket of his blazer with his left hand, pulling out a thin metal box. He flicked up the lid with his thumb and held it out for us to see. There it was, right enough, a hypo, primed and ready. 'I cooked it up in advance,' he said. 'There's enough in there to see you both off, believe me. It's a relic of a rogue consignment I confiscated from a member of the company in Edinburgh last year. The fool was going to take it. It's quite pure, uncut.'

A slow, wicked, leering smile, spread across his face. 'Right, to the performance. Oh, how I love live theatre!

'Let's see. Who goes first?' He looked at us, from me, to Prim, and back again. 'You, Oz, you've drawn the lucky bag. Primavera and I will be your audience. But worry not; it will be only a short time, before you are together again.

'Come here, both of you.' We stepped towards him. Fear was beginning to conquer anger, after all. Death is helluva final, when you look at it up close. He held the box out to Prim, keeping the gun on me.

'Take it,' he said, smoothly. 'Dawn told me that you are a nurse, so find a vein and give him half of the barrel.'

Prim looked mesmerised as she took the syringe from its cottonwool bed. She stared at it as she held it up. She gave it a wee squeeze, like they do in the movies, sending some of the juice spraying upwards. She beckoned me. 'Come here darling,' she said, softly, hypnotically. I felt myself drawn to her. The ice was melted, the hamster had gone. I sensed rather than saw Brooks looking at me, anticipating.

And then, quick as a cat, she jammed the syringe into the fleshy base of his right hand, and started to depress the plunger.

He screamed in pain, and dropped the gun. He stared down in horror as the syringe began to empty. Suddenly he unfroze. He tore his wounded hand away from her and yanked the needle out, throwing it as far from him as he could.

I remember once reading an article by some journalist on the tender topic of male sterilisation. Arguing in favour, he wrote that the after-effects of the procedure were no longer-lasting and no worse than a sharp blow in the stones from a soccer ball. Clearly this was a man who had never played football.

I remember my Dad once saying of an infamous serial killer, 'Hanging's too good for that bastard. It's a good kick in the balls he needs.'

And that, right there in the heart of the Geneva woods, was what I gave Rawdon Brooks, as he stood staring at his hand. Only it wasn't; it was worse than that. I gave him, left, right and centre, the legendary Oz Blackstone toe-poke, which may not look elegant, but when perfectly delivered, as this one was, can send the ball, plural in this case, flying further, straighter and faster than the finest instep delivery. I'll never know for sure, but I like to think that I tore them clean off.

He didn't scream. He howled. It was a primal sound, like a bear with its paw caught in a man-trap. I saw Prim staring at him, her mouth wide open in awe at the depths of his agony.

For good measure, as he stood there, clutching his person, knees turned in in the classic manner, I stuck the head on him. I'm not as good at that as I am at the toe-poke, but this was a pretty fair example. My forehead caught him on the left cheekbone, stunning me slightly and rocking him backwards.

I waited for him to go down, as reason told me he must. I stood back and waited for him to crumple. I mean he was a man, and I'd just nailed him with a blow from which not even the strongest guy can recover.

Yet he was still on his feet, the great bastard. His eyes were rolling, his cheek was swelling, his chest was heaving, but he was still on his feet. He reminded me bizarrely of Charles Laughton after his flogging in *Hunchback*, only Esmeralda was nowhere in sight. As I stood there watching him, I became transfixed. When his hand shot out and caught me round the throat, I didn't move. It wasn't until he began to squeeze that I realised how strong he was. Within a second or two my eyes began to swim. My hands went to his wrist, but his grip was locked on tight.

I was thinking about nothing other than him, and dying. The two muffled plops from my left hardly registered. What *did* register was Brooks' hand loosening its grip as he straightened up and fell backwards. His blazer had fallen open, and I saw the sudden bloom of red on his chest.

I looked behind me. Primavera stood there, as I had never seen her before. Her hands were locked together around the run in a markswoman's grip. Her eyes were cold and hard. And then all at once, they softened, and she started to shake.

I grabbed the gun from her and jammed it into a side pocket of the satchel. On the ground, Brooks rolled over, scrambling around, trying to get to his feet. Christ, was there no stopping this guy!

'Come on!' I yelled at Primavera, dragging her back to the real world. 'Let's go!' I grabbed the satchel, and realised for the first time that I still had that stupid duffel bag slung over my shoulder. I threw it away and grabbed her hand, pulling her behind me as we plunged out of the wood, back towards the green space of the park. For a while I thought we were lost, but at last we saw light ahead. As we cleared the woods, we looked at each other. Behind us we could hear the crashing of pursuit.

'Come on!' said Prim this time. 'Let's get back to the car. He doesn't know where that is, or what it looks like.'

'Can you remember the way?'

'I think so. Come on. Run!' We raced off across the grass, towards the gates. Handicapped as I was by the weight of the bag, I could still keep pace with Prim. Or maybe she was hanging back for me; I didn't have the breath to ask her.

We had turned into the street and were racing along the pavement when I looked back over the fence into the park and saw our pursuer break out of the woods. It wasn't a run as much as a shamble, more like Quasimodo than ever. His left eye was closed tight, and his shirt front was soaked in blood. He was loping along, almost doubled over, but he was loping helluva fast.

'Leg it, for Christ's sake,' I gasped. 'Here comes the Devil and he is pissed off!'

We sprinted through the pedestrians, knocking the wee ones aside, excusing ourselves around others. From the sounds of outrage behind us, I guessed that Brooks was clearing everyone out of his way. 'Why isn't the heroin stopping him, if it was meant to kill us?' I gasped.

'Because I just stuck it in his hand, not in a vein. Just shut up and run!'

When we reached the traffic lights, the pedestrian crossing was showing the red man sign, and the vehicles were flowing fast and freely. I grabbed Prim's hand and tugged her along the pavement, off towards the next corner and Rue Berner, looking, searching as we ran, for a gap in the traffic. At last, a chance appeared. We darted out between two cars, did a frantic shimmy in the middle of the road and made it to the other side.

We stopped, and looked back. Brooks was glaring at us across the street. His good eye looked wild, and his chest was heaving, but his eyes were still dead set on us. 'God, the heroin must be fuelling him,' gasped Prim.

If it was, it made him start straight across the road after us, looking neither right nor left.

If you've ever heard a dog, a big dog, being hit by a vehicle, you never forget the sound. But if you've ever heard the noise of a human being run over by a big vehicle, that's something that will give you nightmares for weeks afterwards.

There's the squeal of brakes and the awful thump, but then there's a tearing, dragging, cracking, crushing sound, and an awful last gasp. We were legging it up the pavement, when we heard it all. Gradually we slowed to a halt, like we were in a film and the camera was breaking down, until, reluctantly, we turned around.

It was a tourist bus, from Bathgate, of all places. When we saw him, Brooks was still moving under its wheels, his head and bloody chest sticking out. The rest of him was hidden, fortunately, under the bus, but around him, a crimson pool was starting to spread.

Instinctively, Primavera started towards him, but I took her hand, holding her back. 'No, honey,' I said, as gently as I could. 'You're not a nurse any more, remember. We've won. Now let's just get ourselves out of here.

'You and I are going home. I don't know about you, but I am absolutely knackered.'

In which the boat sails
and our ship comes in.

We almost melted the wee Peugeot, but we made it to St Malo just in time to catch the night crossing. And this time there was a cabin available; a tiny cabin, but one of our very own, with a shower and two berths.

A Grand Prix circuit: small, but very definitely Formula One.

'Primavera, Primavera . . .' I moaned her name in the dim glow of the emergency light. She leaned her head towards me, kissing my chest, biting my nipples gently, responding to my touch and moving her self against my hands.

'Where have you come from?' I asked, wallowing at last in the perfection of her body, in her firm, full, big-nippled breasts, in the amazing narrowness of her waist, in the rounded curve of her hips, in the flatness of her belly, in the thick nest of wiry blonde hair at her centre, shining and sparkling as she moved.

'I've always been here,' she said, and she kissed me with her lips of velvet, as she had never kissed me before. 'I believe in

239

destiny. You're part of mine, I'm part of yours. We were set on a course towards each other.'

'And will we go on together, we two, Springtime and Oz?'

'Who knows? *Right now* we're together, and that's what counts.'

I crouched above her, burying my face in her belly. As I flicked my tongue in and out of her navel, she gasped and arched her back. 'I want you now. I need you now. Come into me now.'

I placed a finger across her lips. 'Time enough,' I said, although she could feel that I was more than ready. I bent and kissed the inside of her thighs as she spread them wide, licking my way towards her. She moaned again. 'Now, Oz, now.'

'Yes, Primavera, yes!' I covered her and she took me into herself with a supple movement, into the sweetest embrace I had ever known. We lay entwined, barely moving. Her tongue was in my mouth again, her fingers wound through my crinkly hair. She pulled my head back and looked at me with smouldering eyes. 'You pass the audition. The job's yours!' she hissed.

Then her eyelids flickered and she began to shudder, gripping me tight, inside, tighter than I had ever imagined. Her fingers dug into my back, and she cried out, once, twice, again, again, again, again. And then I realised that two voices were calling out and that one of them was mine. I was lost. As I thrust into her and as she grasped me with her thighs and held me there, we were washed, on the high seas, by wave upon wave of sensation, by a feeling that every nerve-ending in our bodies was being bathed in soothing oil.

At last, we lay still. Her eyes were closed, and there was a sheen of sweat on her face. I licked it off; she tasted salty and sublime on my tongue. I felt myself start to subside, but she held me inside her. 'No, don't go,' she sighed. 'I want to keep you there for ever.'

'That's all right with me,' I said. 'I can't think of a better place to be. Primavera Phillips, you are the most beautiful, wonderful woman I have ever met, and I love you.'

She smiled up at me in the darkness, and smoothed damp hair away from my forehead. 'And I love you too, Oz Blackstone,' she murmured. 'It's been a crazy week, but this . . . this is like a dream.'

'Yes,' I said, 'like a dream I've had before.'

In which we find another stiff in Prim's bed, a sort of justice is done and there is a twist in the tale.

We made it back to Edinburgh on Sunday, via Portsmouth and points north, including Peter's hotel in Middleton-One-Row, where the three of us got completely stupid drunk, and, as I recall, Prim and I did something even stupider involving the absence of condoms.

The last few hours of the weekend, we spent tidying up the loft, before we enjoyed the unimaginable luxury of making love and sleeping together in our own bed, even if we did have a clearly contented iguana for company.

Next morning I phoned Archer, got through to him personally and in the most solemn voice I could manage, made an appointment to see him at three-thirty. Then I called Jan, and, putting aside my aversion to pubs at lunchtime, arranged to meet her, and Ellen, and the kids, who were all still at her place, in Whighams at one o'clock. That gave us some time to kill.

'Oz,' said Prim, as we lay in bed, under the light from the belvedere, 'sooner rather than later, I've got to go back to my flat, to pick up the rest of my things.' I didn't want to go back there, and neither did she, but she was right. It had to be done.

It felt strange parking in Ebeneezer Street. It was the place where I'd met Prim, yet I felt uncomfortable, still a stranger. It was *her* turf, not ours.

She must have read my mind. 'Oz, love,' she said as we climbed the dusty stair. 'Would you mind if I sold this place? Or would you think I was rushing things?'

I looked over solemnly. 'Maybe you should hold off,' I said, and then I kissed her. 'Until tomorrow. We've got a few things to do today.'

She unlocked the door and went to step inside, but I held her back. 'Hold on,' I said, laughing. 'Let me check the bed. Just in case there's a body in there.' She grinned as I looked round the bedroom door.

There was a body in the bed. It was Miles Grayson. But it was a brand new bed, and fortunately, he was very much alive. Dawn lay on his far side, hunched down as if she was trying to hide. I don't know which of us went pinker faster. 'I see you took our advice,' I said to her.

'Oz!' said Miles, the sound of his voice bringing Prim bursting into the room. 'Where the hell have you two been? Dawn's been worried about you.'

'So I see,' said Prim, archly, but with a smile.

'We just nipped over to France for a few days. To sort of, get to know each other, like.' A sudden thought struck me. 'Here, while we were away, we had this terrific idea for a film script. Come for dinner tonight and we'll tell you about it. We owe you a beer anyway.'

'Yes,' said Prim to her sister. 'And bring the rest of my clothes while you're at it.'

I flipped a card from the breast pocket of my Savoy Tailors'

Guild suit on to the bed. 'That's where we live. See you tonight. You be bad now!'

The whole team was gathered in Whighams when we got there, filling one of the low alcoves. There was a glass of draught Coke waiting for me, and a glass of white wine for Primavera. She jammed herself into a corner, on the far side of Jan. I sat down between my nephews and my sister and gave them all hugs. 'Everything all right, Ellie?'

She smiled at me. 'We'll see, Oz. We'll see. I'm going to stay at Dad's for a while, to see if I can get something of my old shape back and to see if Allan comes for me. If he does, I'll decide then whether I'll go back or not. The bugger's got to want me though.'

She whispered in my ear. 'Is this it then? Are you happy?'

'Ecstatic.' I whispered back.

'Good. Jan isn't, though.'

'Eh?'

'You don't have a clue about women, do you, son?'

That was too deep for me. I finished my Coke and went up to the bar for another round. As the barman was filling the tray, an Armani suit appeared by my elbow.

'Did you hear about Ricky Ross?' said Dylan, looking uncharacteristically solemn.

I looked at him, puzzled. 'I've been away. What about him?'

'Suspended. See your murder in Ebeneezer Street? It turned out that Ricky was screwing the victim's wife. Now she's been charged with the murder.

'We checked every detail about Ebeneezer Street that night. We found out that our traffic boys handed out a ticket to a car parked on a double yellow line there, just about the time that Kane was killed. It turned out that it belonged to his wife. She admits that she was there, but she swears he was alive when she left. I don't believe her though. We'll see whether the jury does.

'After we pulled her in she screamed bloody murder and shouted for Ricky. When he said he couldn't do anything she told us everything about him and her. He said that he'd encouraged her to leave the wee chap, and that he'd been blazing when she said she wanted him back. She even suggested that he might have done the murder.

'There's nothing to substantiate that, but being implicated in a murder inquiry's enough. He's out, and that's for sure.

'I'll tell you something, Blackstone, just between you and me. If you ever repeat it, I'll deny it all. Ricky really fancied you for it. He thought that you and the actress girl had set it up between you.'

His voice dropped to a whisper. 'You had a break-in at your flat, aye?'

I nodded, wondering. 'That was Ricky,' he said. 'I nearly shit myself when he told me he'd done that.'

'Nice of him. I don't feel sorry for him now. Here, I hope we're in the clear now. Ricky's theory was pure mince, you know.'

Dylan smiled again. 'Aye, you're okay. The Chief sorted him out on that. Your girlfriend's sister's in Miles Grayson's film, isn't she?'

'That's right.'

'Aye well, Sir James had a phone call last Monday evening, from Grayson. His secretary told me. She said that Grayson sounded really steamed up. The call lasted for about five minutes. When it was over, the Chief called Ricky in and sorted him out.'

I smiled at him. 'See truth, eh? Stranger than fiction.

246

'Here, Mike, did you ever find that fiver? The one that Prim spent.'

He laughed. 'You bugger! Aye; at least we think we did. We checked everything in town that looked like a grocer, and eventually we found a Bank of Scotland Fiver torn in two and taped back together in a place off Broughton Street. Is that where she spent it?'

I shrugged my shoulders. 'I wouldn't know. I wasn't with her all the time. What was your problem about that anyway?'

Dylan glowered. 'The Chief started that panic off too. He did a snap inspection of CID. Some stupid bastard of a DC let slip about your girlfriend picking up the fiver and the old fella tore Ricky up in front of everyone. So when he'd gone, Ricky put the·thumbscrews on me. I'll tell you, if I hadn't found it, I'd have been back in uniform.'

I shook my head at the poor dupe. He hadn't even had the wit to take another fiver and cut it in half. I felt sorry for him. 'Here's a tip for you, then, to make up for it. Someone tried to kill my girlfriend's sister the Sunday before last. Hit and run, up in Auchterarder. The trouble is, outside the family the only people who knew that she was there were the film crew, and the police.

'We didn't report it, because she's in the movie and couldn't stand the publicity. But just for fun, why don't you check the car-hire companies and see whether anyone hired a medium-sized navy blue or black saloon, maybe a Mondeo, that day, then brought it back damaged, either very late at night or first thing next morning. I'll bet you'll find someone did, and that it was Linda Kane. Dig deeper and I think you'll find that Ricky told her that Dawn was at her folks' place.'

He looked at me, crest well fallen. 'Cheers Mike,' I said, and carried my tray back to the table.

And that was it. When we'd finished our drinks, Jan, Ellen and I had a mass exchange of car keys, then Prim and I went off for a reunion with the Nissan, which Jan had parked on the west side of Charlotte Square, only a hundred yards from the pub.

I was going to walk to Black and Muirton's but Prim said, 'No. Not with all that cash.' So we drove round the square and off along George Street. I ask you, who ever finds a parking space in George Street in the middle of the afternoon? We were all the way down in Heriot Row before I spotted a vacant bay.

'Right waste of time that was. I've got as far to walk back,' I said, jerking on the handbrake, and reaching into the back seat for the satchel of cash.

It felt cold and hard against my ribs. Gun barrels do, being metal and all. When they've a big silencer on them, it's even worse.

I looked into her eyes, saw myself reflected in them and knew what yet another word looked like. This time it was 'incredulous'. It's the look that comes with discovering that, however well you *think* you know someone, however close you are, you can never know them completely, never get completely inside their head.

'I'm sorry, Oz,' she said, quietly, almost tearfully, 'but I just can't let you.'

'Prim.' It came out as a croak. 'What do you mean?'

'I mean, my lover, that you and I are not as alike as you think. I know that not once have you ever thought of the possibility of just holding on to all of that untraceable cash, and using it to shape the rest of our lives.

'On the other hand, since I put those two bullets into old Rawdon, I've thought of nothing else. And even before then, the notion was more than tickling my fancy, it was giving me orgasms.'

I let go of the bag, dropping it back on to the seat. 'Come on Prim. Isn't a half-share of ninety thousand enough.'

She shook her head. 'No it bloody well isn't. I told you right at the start, five per cent wouldn't do.'

I looked down at the gun. I don't know much about safety catches, and I hadn't a clue whether this one was on or off. I slipped my left hand round her shoulders but she pulled back, digging the silencer in even harder. 'I mean it Oz. I can't let you do it. We were nearly killed for that money, and I shot a man because of it. It's gone past the stage of being someone's possession. It's a prize and we've won it.'

I looked at her, afraid to ask her just one question. 'And would you shoot me to keep it?' I'd seen enough lawyers in action to know that you never put a question to a witness unless you were certain of the answer.

So instead I said. 'You really mean it?'

She nodded. 'Yes,' she said, in a quiet voice.

'You're saying you want us to tell Archer that someone beat us to it, then take all of this untraceable money and bugger off somewhere warm for a few years, secure in the knowledge that even if he twigs, he won't be able to do anything about it other than watch his ship sink or have a whip-round among the boys to cover the loss.

'Is that what you're saying?'

'Yes.' It was barely a whisper now.

I looked at her, long and hard. I was really angry with her, for the first time in my life.

'In that case,' I said, slowly and evenly, 'what the hell d'you need the gun for?'

Her smile, her wonderful smile, flooded across her face.

She took the automatic from my ribs, held it up, pulled the magazine from the butt and showed it to me. It was empty.

I glowered at her. 'There's just one thing,' I grunted.

'What's that?' she said leaning forward and kissing me.

'Wherever we go, Wallace goes with us!'